Reprinted in 2016 by

An imprint of Om Books International

Corporate & Editorial Office
A 12, Sector 64, Noida 201 301
Uttar Pradesh, India
Phone: +91 120 477 4100
Email: editorial@ombooks.com
Website: www.ombooksinternational.com

Sales Office
107, Ansari Road, Darya Ganj,
New Delhi 110 002, India
Phone: +91 11 4000 9000, 2326 3363, 2326 5303
Fax: +91 11 2327 8091
Email: sales@ombooks.com
Website: www.ombooks.com

ISBN: 978-93-80070-83-4

Printed in India

10 9 8 7 6 5 4

365 STORIES FOR BOYS

OM KIDZ

An imprint of Om Books International

Contents

MAY

APRIL

OCTOBER

SEPTEMBER

Diogenes and the Ferryman 208
True and False Dreams 209
A Crocodile and a Fisherman 209

NOVEMBER

DECEMBER

1. Hans in Luck

Hans was a cheerful boy. He had happily served his master for seven years. Now, Hans left for home. As a farewell gift, his master gave him a lump of gold. During his journey, Hans met a horseman. Seeing the man ride merrily, Hans exchanged his gold for the horse and trotted away. However, when Hans pushed the horse to run faster, he was thrown off.

Then, Hans saw a countryman with a cow. Hans traded his horse for the cow. After some time, Hans stopped at a moor to milk the cow. A butcher passing by told Hans that his cow was too old to be milked. Hans took the butcher's pig in exchange for his cow.

Next, Hans met a mason and exchanged his pig with the mason's grindstones. The heavy stones soon tired Hans. He went to a well to drink water and dropped the stones inside by mistake! Hans ran home, empty-handed but still happy.

2. Faithful John

Once, a king fell very ill. Before dying, he said to his faithful servant, "John! I leave you with a very important task. My son is young. I want you to be his guardian." John nodded his head, his eyes wet with tears. The prince fell in love with a princess. They decided to marry.

One day, John overheard three divine ravens make some predictions. One of them said, "If the prince mounts his horse, a curse will befall him. If someone else kills the horse, the prince will be saved."

The second raven added, "The prince will see a bridegroom dress. If he wears it, his body would melt away. Somebody will have to throw the dress into the fire."

The third raven said, "When the prince dances with the princess, the princess will turn pale. If someone does not kiss her, she will die. If somebody shares these spells with the prince, he will turn into a stone statue."

John decided to sacrifice his life for the prince. He killed the horse and threw the bridegroom's dress in the fire. But when he kissed the princess, the prince sentenced him to death.

John then told him all about the predictions. The prince felt sorry as John turned into a stone statue!

Soon, the prince and his wife were blessed with twin boys. They wished John could come back to life. One day, the statue spoke, "Master! I can come back to life if you sacrifice your twin sons."

The prince was confused and sad. He then decided to pay back John's loyalties. The prince was about to cut his sons' heads when John came back to life. He said, "Master! God has heard your prayers of repentance and sacrifice. I shall always serve you now."

3. Brother Lustig

Brother Lustig was a poor, but kind man. Once he helped a beggar. Now, this was St. Peter in disguise! St. Peter felt sad for Brother Lustig's poverty, so he decided to help him. He would cure people to earn money for Brother Lustig and himself. Now, the king's daughter fell ill. St. Peter placed his hand on her and cured her. He refused the reward for it, but Brother Lustig became greedy and took the money. St. Peter felt sad at this and left Brother Lustig.

Some days later, Lustig tried to cure another princess by himself. He placed his hand on her head but she lay motionless. Magically, St. Peter appeared. He promised to revive her if Lustig stopped being greedy. Brother Lustig agreed at once. St. Peter cured her. Then, he gave Lustig a bag, which had many medicines. With those medicines, Lustig could now cure people and earn an honest living.

4. The Willow-wren and the Bear

One day, a bear and a wolf heard a bird singing. The bear asked the wolf, "Who is singing so well?" "The King of Birds," replied the wolf. The bear saw the nest and the baby willow-wrens and said, "King of Birds! But this is neither a royal palace nor are these birds of good breed."

This upset the tiny baby willow-wrens. They started crying and refused to eat. Father willow-wren was so angry that he declared war against the bear. The fox was to lead the animal's army. As long as his bushy tail was lifted, they were to fight, and if it was down they were to run away.

The battle began between the animals and the birds. A hornet stung the fox under his tail. The fox lowered his tail in pain. Thus, the enemy ran away! And the defeated bear had to apologise to the willow-wrens.

5. The Shroud

Once upon a time, there lived a mother and her son. The little boy was very handsome and loved by all. The mother adored him. One day, the boy fell ill and died. The mother was shattered.

Then the boy appeared at night in the places where he played, when he was alive. He would see his mother cry, and would disappear before the morning.

The mother would not stop crying. One night, the boy appeared in the same shroud and wreath in which he was buried and said, "Oh, Mother, please stop crying, or I shall never fall asleep. For my shroud will not dry because of all your tears."

From that night on, she wept no more. The next night, the little boy appeared again and said, "Look, Mother, my shroud is nearly dry, I will soon rest." The mother was now consoled and the child appeared no more.

6. The Straw, the Coal and the Bean

One day, a poor old woman wanted to cook some beans. She made a fire with straw and coal. While emptying the beans into the pan, one bean dropped on the ground beside a straw. Soon, a burning coal from the fire fell near them.

The straw said, "Friends, we are lucky to have escaped death here. Let's go away to a safer place." Thus, they set out together.

Soon, they came to a little brook. The straw suggested, "I will lay myself straight across, and you use me as a bridge." The coal started to walk on the straw. Midway, she got scared and could not move. The coal's heat burnt the straw and they both fell down and drowned in the brook.

Seeing this, the bean laughed so hard that she burst. Luckily, a tailor saw her, and sewed her together using black thread. So, all beans since then have a black stitch!

7. Bearskin

One day, a brave soldier met a stranger in a green coat. The stranger said, "I can make you happy. But you can neither stay at one place, nor bathe or cut your hair and nails for seven years." Before going away, the stranger gave the soldier his green coat and a bearskin to wear and some money to travel. The soldier, now called Bearskin, travelled around the world and grew dirty and ugly every day.

Once, Bearskin helped a needy old man, who offered Bearskin one of his beautiful daughters' hand in marriage. The old man's youngest daughter agreed to marry Bearskin. However, Bearskin had to continue his travels. But before leaving, he broke his ring in two, and gave the girl one half of the ring and left with the other.

At the end of seven years, the handsome soldier returned and showed the girl his half of the ring. The soldier and the girl were married and lived happily ever after.

8. The Godfather

Once, a poor man had so many children that he had asked all his relatives to be his children's godparents.

Now he wondered who could be the new baby's godparent! Soon, he fell asleep and dreamt that he should ask the first person he met to be the godparent. He woke up and went out. He met a stranger and requested him to be the godparent. The stranger agreed and gave him some healing water, which could cure people.

The man took the water and cured the sick and became very rich. The man then went to meet the godparent to thank him. However, when he entered the godparent's house, he saw that the godparent had wings. He had the head of a man and the body of a horse!

Then the man understood that the godparent was actually God's kind angel who had come to earth!

9. The Fearless Prince

Once, there was a fearless young prince, who set out on an adventure. While travelling, he reached a giant's castle. The giant caught him and sent him to fetch a magic apple. The brave prince brought back the magical apple and gave it to the giant.

During his journey, the prince had become friendly with a lion, who had given him a magical ring. Now, the greedy giant wanted the ring, too, but the prince refused to give it. The giant tricked the prince into a fight. However, the lion saved the prince and killed the giant.

The prince carried on with his journey. Soon, he reached a mansion where a cursed princess was locked. To save the princess, the prince stayed up for three nights in the haunted mansion. He suffered much torture by the ghosts of the mansion, but finally saved the princess.

The prince returned home with the princess and lived happily ever after.

10. Fundevogel

Once, a carpenter found a boy in the forest. He took the boy home and named him Fundevogel. The carpenter's daughter, Lina, and Fundevogel grew fond of each other. Now, Fundevogel had magical powers. But their cook was envious of Fundevogel.

One day, she told a maid to throw Fundevogel into boiling water. However, Lina heard them and she and Fundevogel escaped together from the house.

The cook sent three servants after them. But, Lina and Fundevogel fooled them twice by changing their form through magic. First, they became a rose tree with Lina the rose and then a church with Lina, the chandelier.

The cook decided to catch them herself. Then, Fundevogel turned into a pond and Lina, the duck. The cook understood their plan. She tried to drink the water but the duck held her head under water and she drowned. Lina and Fundevogel lived happily thereafter.

11. Cat and Mouse

Once, a cat and a mouse were good friends. One day, they decided to save some food for winter. Thus, they stole a pot of fat and hid it in a church.

Now, the greedy cat wanted to eat the fat. So, she lied to the mouse, "I've been invited to the church for a christening!" Then, she ate the fat off the top of the pot. When she returned, she told the mouse that the baby was named Top-Off. The second time, she ate half the fat, and told the mouse that the baby was named Half-Done. The third time, she ate all the fat, and said that the baby's name was All-Gone.

When winter came, the two went to get the pot of fat. The mouse saw the empty pot and said angrily, "Now I understand the meaning of those names!" But the cat jumped on the mouse and ate him too.

12. The Lonely Musician

Once, a musician was walking through a forest. He felt very lonely and thought, "I need a companion."

Then, he started playing his merry fiddle. A wolf heard him and said, "Lovely! Can I accompany you?" The musician understood that the wolf would eat him. Thus, he tricked the wolf to get stuck in an oak tree.

The musician played again, and a fox came. Now, he didn't want the fox to walk with him. Thus, he left the fox hanging from a hazel-bush. Next, came a hare but the musician tied it to an aspen tree.

Soon, a woodcutter heard the musician play and came. "Ah! The perfect companion at last," thought the musician. Meanwhile, the wolf, the fox and the hare escaped and came after the musician. However, the woodcutter chased them away with his axe.

The musician gratefully played for the woodcutter, while they walked together through the forest.

13. The Ragamuffins

One day, a cock and a hen went to a hill to eat nuts. After eating nuts the whole day, they decided to go home in a carriage of nutshells. Then, a duck came and said, "You stole my nuts!" The cock fought and defeated the duck and made him pull the carriage.

On the way, they met a needle and a pin, who took a ride in their carriage. They travelled together and reached an inn. The cock said to the innkeeper, "Let us stay for a night. In return, you can keep the hen's egg and the duck."

The cock and the hen woke up early, and put the eggshell in the Innkeeper's hearth. They put the pin on the innkeeper's towel and the needle on his cushion. Then, they went away without paying. So did the duck.

In the morning, the innkeeper got hurt by the eggshell, the pin and the needle. He vowed never to take such ragamuffins into his house again!

14. The King of the Golden Mountain

Once, there was a merchant who had lost his ships at sea. As he stood unhappily near a stream, a dwarf appeared before him.

The dwarf promised him great riches. In exchange, he wanted the merchant's beloved son after twelve years. The merchant agreed thinking the dwarf's promise to be false. However, when he returned home, he found a heap of gold coins in his cupboard. He was rich again.

Twelve years went by. It was time to repay the dwarf. The young son heard of his father's promise. He went fearlessly to meet the dwarf.

The dwarf asked the young boy to sit in a boat. The helpless merchant watched as the boat disappeared down the stream. The boat reappeared on an unknown shore with a beautiful castle. In the castle, the young boy met a beautiful princess. He married her and became the king of the Golden Mountain.

15. The Cat Princess

Once, there lived an old miller, who had three helpers. The old miller said, "I am old, and want to retire. Whoever brings me the best horse shall have the mill and also take care of me."

The three boys left in search of horses. One of them got lost and found himself in a cave. The cave belonged to a cat. The cat said, "If you serve me for seven years, your wish will be fulfilled."

The boy went with the cat and obeyed her orders. He even built a beautiful house for her. Seven years passed and the boy returned to the miller. The cat said she would follow him to the mill with his horse.

One day, a beautiful coach arrived at the mill with a princess. This was the cat! The princess gave the old miller the horse and got married to the boy.

16. The Ungrateful Son

Once, there lived a mean and selfish man with his wife. One evening, they were eating a roasted chicken. Just then, through the window, he saw his father coming. He did not want to share the chicken with him and hid it under the table. The father just took a drink and went away.

The man then took the chicken out but it had changed into a big ugly toad. The toad jumped and sat on the man's face. From then onwards, the toad stayed there always. If anyone tried to take it off the man's face, the toad scared them. It would act as if it would jump on them.

This ungrateful son was taught a lesson! He had to feed the toad every day. If he forgot to do so, the toad snatched his food. The man had to live forever with the toad on his face!

17. The Young Giant

Once, there lived a farmer. He had a tiny son, no bigger than his thumb. One day, the farmer went to plough his field. His son wanted to come along. The farmer was afraid to take him. However, the son cried and so he took him.

On the field, a giant came and took away the tiny son. The helpless farmer tried to put up a fight, but could not stop the giant.

The giant looked after the boy for many years. The boy grew into a young giant. One day, he wanted to return to his father. He set off for his land. The farmer was speechless to see the young giant.

The giant told the old farmer that he was his son. Then, he took the furrow from his father. He ploughed the large field. The young giant was hungry after work. They returned home together for rest. The little boy was now a man. He was a good son to his old father.

18. Poverty and Humility

There was once a prince who was thoughtful and sad. Once, he saw a monk and asked him, "How can I reach Heaven?" The monk answered, "By poverty and humility."

The prince wore a monk's garments and left home. He travelled all around and suffered misery, but prayed every day. He returned to his palace after seven years, but no one recognised him. Out of pity, the Queen granted him a place under the stairs and two meals a day.

The prince was sick, and grew weaker. As the prince's illness increased, he desired to receive the last sacrament. After the prayers, when the priest went to him, he lay dead.

The prince had a rose in one hand and a lily in the other. Beside him was a paper with his story. When he was buried, a rose grew on one side of his grave, and a lily on the other.

19. The Twelve Apostles

Three hundred years before the birth of Lord Christ, there lived a poor woman who had twelve sons. She prayed to God daily that he would grant her sons to be on Earth with the promised Saviour. However, her poverty forced her to send them, one after the other, out into the world to earn their livelihood.

The eldest son, Peter, after walking for a whole day, got lost. As he lay dying, suddenly, a small angelic boy who shone with brightness appeared before him. The boy took Peter to a cavern that had twelve golden cradles, and asked Peter to sleep in one of them.

One after the other, all the twelve brothers came and lay there sleeping in the golden cradles. They slept for three hundred years, until the night when the Saviour was born. Then they awoke, and were with him on Earth, and were called the Twelve Apostles.

20. Three Green Leaves

Once, there was a hermit who was kind and holy. An angel accompanied him and fed him. One day, the hermit saw a sinner being taken to be hanged, and said, "He is getting what he deserves." God became angry with him because he spoke harshly about the sinner. The angel said, "Take this dry branch, and live like a beggar. God will forgive your sin when three green leaves appear on it."

The hermit went out into the world with the dry branch and became a beggar. One day, he found an old woman with three sons who were robbers. When the hermit told his story to them, the robbers were shocked, and sincerely repented for their lifetime of crimes.

In the morning, they found the hermit dead. However there were three green leaves on the dry branch. Thus, God forgave the hermit and took him to Heaven.

21. The Four Friends

Once there were four friends – a donkey, a dog, a cat and a cock. When they became old, their masters decided to kill them. And so, they decided to run away. On their way, it became dark. They decided to rest in a forest. The cock saw the light of a house in the distance. The four friends started walking towards the house.

When they reached there, they saw a group of thieves gathered around a table piled with food. The four friends were very hungry. They started singing loudly. The thieves thought that they were ghosts and got frightened.

However, the leader of the thieves was not frightened. He sent one of his men to examine the house. The four friends pounced on the thief and beat him up.

All the thieves ran away in fear, believing that the house was haunted. The four friends lived there happily ever after.

22. The Peasant's Wife

Once, a peasant was going on a journey. He said to his wife, "You have to sell these three cows for a good price when I am away, or else you will be punished."

The next morning, the cattle-dealer agreed to pay a good price but had forgotten his purse. The peasant's wife insisted the payment be made in full in exchange for the cows.

The cattle-dealer said, "I shall leave one cow behind, and when I return with the money for the three cows, I shall take the third as well."

The peasant returned and was very angry with the arrangement. He decided to spare his wife only if he found someone more foolish than her. Soon he met a woman whom he fooled by saying he had dropped from heaven. The woman believed him and gave some money for her dead husband.

The peasant took the money and went home. He then spared his wife!

23. The Water of Life

Once, there was a king. He was dying. His worried son met a wise old man. He told the prince that the Water of Life could save his father. The prince went in search of it.

On the way, a dwarf stopped the prince. The prince told the dwarf about his sick father and begged him for help. The kind dwarf said, "The Water of Life is in a magical fountain in the enchanted castle. Take this wand and a loaf of bread; they will help you."

The prince reached the enchanted castle. He tapped on the door with the wand. It opened and he saw a lion sitting inside. He threw the bread to the lion. After eating it, the lion fell asleep. Then, he collected the Water from the magical fountain.

Quickly, he rode back to his father. The king recovered after drinking the water and thanked his brave son.

24. The Spirit in the Bottle

Once, there was a poor woodcutter. His son was very clever. Sadly, the boy had to quit school as they were poor. Now, he had to go to the forest with his father to chop wood.

One day, the woodcutter was resting and the boy wandered around in the forest. Just then, he heard a voice calling out from the roots of an oak tree. He dug the earth near the roots and found a spirit inside a bottle.

The spirit begged to be released. The boy opened the bottle and the spirit flew out. The spirit was grateful on being freed. He offered the boy a reward, a magic rag. The rag could heal any wound that it covered. On rubbing iron or a metal with the rag, it turned into silver.

Since then, the woodcutter became very rich. And, the boy joined school again. He went on to become a famous doctor.

25. Hans' Patches

Hans was a young peasant. His Uncle Tom wanted to find him a rich wife. He went to the nearby village, wearing an old, patched coat. There, Uncle Tom met a rich man and his daughter. He told them that Hans was an honest and sensible man. The rich man asked, "Does Hans have any patches of land?"

Uncle Tom was smart. He hit the patches on his torn coat and said, "Hans has more patches than me." The rich man thought he meant patches of land. He wanted his daughter to be richer. Thus, he wanted her to marry Hans.

Soon, they were married. After the wedding, Hans and his wife walked in the fields. He wore his torn coat with the patches. He explained that he had many patches on his coat but none of the land. Hans' wife was happy to see his honesty and lived happily ever after.

26. Herr Korbes

Once, a hen and a cock decided to take revenge on a man called Herr Korbes. They set off in a carriage built by the cock and pulled by mice.

On their way, they met a cat who wanted to know where they were going. The cock told him, "To the house of Herr Korbes." The cat wanted to go, too, so he sat at the back of the carriage.

Soon, a big millstone, an egg, a duck, a pin and a needle came aboard. They also wanted to go to Herr Korbes' house. They reached his house and all of them placed themselves in various places.

Finally, Herr Korbes came home. He was attacked by the visitors and hurt very badly. Just as he was about to leave his house, very angry, the millstone fell on him and he got a bump on his head. Surely, Herr Korbes must have been a very wicked man!

27. The Cobbler and the Elves

Once, there was a poor cobbler. He had only enough leather to make one pair of shoes. So he cut out the leather and went to sleep.

In the morning, he saw a fine pair of shoes. Soon after, a customer paid the cobbler good money for the beautiful shoes. The cobbler bought enough leather for two pairs of shoes with the money. And, the next morning, two beautiful pairs of shoes were ready!

This went on till finally the cobbler and his wife decided to hide and watch what happened in the night. They then saw two poorly dressed elves make the shoes.

In gratitude, the wife stitched some clothes for the elves. At night, the couple placed the clothes on the table and hid themselves. The elves came in through the window. They saw the new clothes and were overjoyed.

After that night, the elves never came again. However, the cobbler became rich and happy.

28. Old Sultan

There was once a wise dog named Sultan. He was growing old, so his master wanted to shoot him. Sultan made a plan with his friend, the wolf. The wolf pretended to steal the child of Sultan's master. Sultan saved the child and earned his master's trust. Now, the wolf wanted Sultan to allow him to steal some sheep from his master's flock. However, Sultan told his master about the wolf's plan. The master caught the wolf and beat him up.

The wolf was very angry with Sultan, so, he called Sultan to the forest. He also called the wild boar to teach Sultan a lesson. Sultan went to the forest with a three-legged cat. The wolf and the boar were scared of the strange cat. They ran in fear but the cat bit the boar's ear. The wolf at once made peace with Sultan. Sultan lived happily ever after.

29. The Wedding of Mrs. Fox

Once, there was an old fox that had nine tails. He thought that his wife was not faithful to him. Thus, one day, to test her, the fox lay down on a bench and played dead. When Mrs. Fox saw him, she shut herself in her room and refused to come out.

Soon, a young fox came to meet Mrs. Fox. He wanted to marry her. However, Mrs. Fox was not interested in him as he had only one tail. She wanted to marry someone with nine tails.

Many suitors came; each with one tail more than the previous, but Mrs. Fox did not accept. Finally, a young fox with nine tails approached her and she immediately agreed to marry him.

However, just as the ceremonies began, Mr. Fox jumped up and swung his club at the guests. He also chased Mrs. Fox and her fiancé out of the house!

30. The Tailor in Heaven

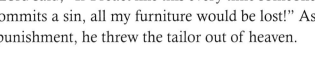

In heaven, one day, God decided to take a walk. He took all the saints with him. He left Saint Peter behind and instructed him not to let anyone in.

Soon, a poor tailor knocked on the Pearly Gates. Saint Peter felt sorry for him and let him in. He said, "Sit behind the gate quietly." However, when Peter was not looking, the tailor went and sat on the Lord's throne.

From Heaven, he saw a woman on Earth stealing, and in his fury, he threw a footstool at her. He then realised his folly and returned to his assigned seat. Soon, the Lord returned. He saw that his footstool was missing and caught the tailor.

The tailor narrated what happened. The Lord said, "If I react like this every time someone commits a sin, all my furniture would be lost!" As a punishment, he threw the tailor out of heaven.

31. The Sun Brings It to Light

Once, a poor tailor went out looking for work. On the way, he met a man, who had lots of money. The tailor beat him up and took away all his money. Just before the tailor left, the man said, "The bright sun will bring it to light."

The tailor went on his way. Soon, the tailor found work and later married his master's daughter.

One morning, as the tailor was having his coffee, the sun shone on the coffee and reflected in circles on the wall. This reminded him of what the man had said. His wife saw him worried and urged him to tell her the reason.

The tailor explained the whole incident and pleaded her to keep it a secret. However, his wife shared it with her best friend. Soon all the villagers came to know, too. The tailor was put on trial and then sent to prison.

1. The Peasant Who Fooled the Devil

One evening, a peasant was working in his field. He suddenly saw a burning heap of coals. A cheeky little Devil sat on them.

"You are in my field," the peasant said.

"Ah, but there's treasure in it," said the Devil. "You can reach it only if you give me whatever grows above the ground."

"Alright," said the cunning peasant, and he grew turnips in his field. Later, when the Devil came to collect his share, he was rudely surprised. He got only leaves as the turnips were below the ground.

"Next harvest, I want what's below the ground," growled the Devil.

The peasant readily agreed. In the next harvest season, he grew wheat. The Devil got only the leaves as wheat grows above the ground!

The Devil was so annoyed that he disappeared in a puff of smoke. The peasant dug up the treasure and went home. He was pleased that he had fooled the Devil!

2. Master Pfriem

Master Pfriem was a cobbler. He was a short and fat man with grey hair. He meddled in everyone else's business, even though he kept busy in his shoe shop. He loved to find fault with everything. He thought that he was always right.

One morning, Master Pfriem woke up and saw that his wife had lit the fire. He rushed to put it out, saying, "The whole house will burn down!" Then, he gobbled his breakfast and ran to his shop.

While Master Pfriem worked on a shoe, his restless eyes looked towards the road. His assistant showed him a shoe. "Bad work," said Master Pfriem.

"Sir, you made it," the assistant said and received a blow behind his ears. None of the assistants worked for more than a month with him!

Then, Master Pfriem saw a crooked beam inserted in the new house being built across the road. He rushed to advise the carpenters. In between, he shouted at a cart-man for overloading his horses. Then, he ran across the road, waving his arms and knocked over a flower-seller's basket. He kept running to correct some other mistake he had spotted.

That night, Master Pfriem dreamed that he was in Heaven. St. Peter allowed him in, saying, "You have a bad habit of finding fault. Don't do it here or you will have to leave." Master Pfriem agreed and wandered around, admiring Heaven and the angels.

Heaven was a busy place. Master Pfriem noticed many things that annoyed him, but he kept quiet. He lost control when he saw two horses harnessed behind a carriage. He shouted, "Stop! This is all wrong!" The next moment Master Pfriem found himself standing outside Heaven's gates.

Right then, he woke up, muttering, "Stupid way to harness horses! But Thank God, I am alive!"

3. The Wise Boy

Once, a king called a boy to his court to test his intelligence. The king asked, "How many drops are there in the ocean?" The boy replied, "Your Majesty, if you stop the new drops of water to enter the ocean, I can easily count the present."

The king then asked, "How many stars are there in the sky?" The boy made countless points on a piece of paper. Then, he said, "If you can count these points then that would be the number of stars in the sky."

At last, the king asked him the number of seconds in eternity. The boy answered, "When a bird sharpens its beak on a two-mile wide, two-mile deep and two-mile high diamond rock, and the rock completely wears off, then the first second of eternity is over."

The king was so happy with the boy that he made him a prince.

4. Two Brothers

Once, two brothers lived in a village. One day, the younger brother went to the forest and brought home a beautiful golden bird. His elder brother got very jealous.

Then, he overheard the younger brother tell his wife, "If someone ate the bird's heart, he would find two gold coins under his pillow every morning."

So, the elder brother stole the bird. His wife cooked it immediately so that he could eat it. She put it in a pot in the kitchen. Just then, the younger brother's children came to the kitchen. They were hungry and all of them ate the cooked bird.

The next day, the younger brother found gold coins under their pillows. The elder brother saw this and blamed his wife. His wife said, "It was your younger brother's destiny to get rich. You can steal the bird but not change what God plans for us."

5. The Rose Elf

Once, an elf lived inside the petals of a rose. One day, he saw a lady kissing her beloved goodbye and the beloved giving her a rose. The elf at once flew into its petals. The lady took the rose home and planted it in a pot.

Now, the lady's brother did not like the man. So, he followed the man, kidnapped him, and threw him in a dungeon.

The elf informed the lady in a dream about this terrible happening. The lady was very sad. She looked of her lover everywhere but could not find him. She was so heartbroken that one day she died. The wicked brother took the rose plant to his room.

The elf told every flower about the cruel brother. That night, invisible spirits appeared from the other plants and beat up the brother. Everyone came to know how wicked the brother was and the lady's beloved was set free from the dungeon.

6. An Evil Looking Glass

Once upon a time, there lived a wicked elf. One day, he was in a good mood. He made a looking glass. It had the power of making anything beautiful that reflected on it, look ugly and frightening. The elf thought it was very funny.

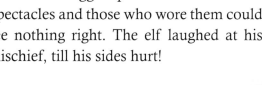

Everybody thought it was a wonderful invention. For the first time, the real nature of people could be known. The people carried the looking glass everywhere. They even wanted to take it to heaven for the angels. However, it slipped and broke into many pieces.

Even the smallest piece had the power of the glass. Some pieces got stuck in the eyes of the people, and they saw things unjustly. Some pieces got stuck to their hearts, which became cold as ice.

The bigger pieces were used as spectacles and those who wore them could see nothing right. The elf laughed at his mischief, till his sides hurt!

7. A Little Boy and the Snow Queen

Once there lived a little boy and girl whose houses were opposite each other. They were very fond of each other. In summer, they would jump out of their windows and play with each other. However, in winter they had to go down the stairs and through the snow to be with each other.

Between their houses were wooden boxes. Beautiful roses grew in them. One winter, the children watched the snowflakes through the window. They thought they were snow bees and wondered if they had a queen.

One day, the Snow Queen waved at the boy through the window. Suddenly he felt a prick in his heart and eye. It was a piece of the magic mirror. His heart became cold as ice and he began seeing everything ugly. He plucked the roses and teased everyone. Then he took his sledge and went to live with the Snow Queen.

8. The Queen Duck

Long ago, there lived a king with his three sons. One day, a neighbouring king visited him. This king's kingdom had turned to stone under a witch's spell.

The king sent his sons to find the key to break the spell. The sons wandered in the forest but could not find it. Wandering, they reached a lake. There were many beautiful ducks playing and swimming in the lake. The first two sons wanted to kill ducks to eat them.

However, the third son said, "I will not let you kill these innocent ducks." They got annoyed and left him alone. The queen duck heard them and went to the third son. She said, "I am indebted to you. So, I will help you find the key."

She got the key from the bottom of the lake and gave it to him. The third son went back and gave the key to his father. The father was very happy, and so was the neighbouring king!

9. Hans, the Hedgehog

Once, a peasant had a son, who was a hedgehog in the upper part of his body and a boy in the lower. His name was Hans, the hedgehog.

One day, the peasant bought a bagpipe for Hans. Hans took his bagpipe and left home forever. Soon, Hans reached a forest. He sat on a tree and played beautiful music.

One day, a king lost his way in the forest. He heard the beautiful music. Then, he saw Hans on the tree and asked for his help. Hans said, "I will help you; but first promise that you would marry your daughter to me."

The king was scared that the forest animals would kill him, and so agreed. Hans guided the king to his kingdom. The grateful king married the princess to Hans.

At night, Hans changed into a handsome man. From then on, he lived happily ever after with the princess.

10. The Two Travellers

Once there lived a very wicked shoemaker and a hardworking tailor. They decided to travel together to a bigger city for better earnings.

Now, the tailor always got jobs wherever they went. The shoemaker was very jealous. Once, the two travellers were crossing a forest. The wicked shoemaker stole the tailor's food and said, "I will share my food with you only if you put chilli in your eyes!"

The poor tailor's went blind because of chilli. The shoemaker left the blind tailor and went away. The tailor had heard that the dew of the night cured blindness. He applied the dew and could see again.

Now, both the shoemaker and the tailor got jobs in the palace. The jealous shoemaker tried to get the tailor into trouble. However, the tailor was so good that the princess decided to marry him! And the shoemaker had to make the wedding shoes!

11. The Dog and the Sparrow

Once, there was a dog, whose master ill-treated him. And so, he ran away, far into the deep forest. There, a kind sparrow helped him find food to eat and found him a nice little cave to make his home in. The dog began to lead a happy life and he and the sparrow became the best of friends. Now, there lived a fox that loved the taste of sparrows and decided to make a meal of the dog's dear friend. So one day, the fox went up to the sparrow and asked her to join her on a walk around the forest to enjoy the lovely weather. Little did she know that the dog was resting in some bushes right next to the tree. The minute he heard the fox utter her sugar-coated lies to coax the sparrow, he pounced on the fox and gave her a sound beating. The fox never dared to trouble the sparrow again.

12. The Wolf and the Man

Once, a wolf and a fox were talking. The wolf did not believe that man could be stronger than him. He asked the fox to show him any man stronger than him.

The next morning, the fox and the wolf waited by the side of a road, where hunters often crossed. Soon a hunter passed by. The fox said, "This is a man. Now, attack him, and prove that you are stronger than him."

The wolf approached the hunter, who shot a bullet at the wolf. The wolf was taken aback but continued his attack. The hunter shot at him again, but the wolf controlled his pain and pursued further.

The hunter then took out a small sword and gave him a few cuts. In pain, the wolf ran back to the fox and narrated what had happened.

The fox then said to him, "You are so proud! You could not swallow your false pride and almost got killed." The wolf admitted that man was stronger.

13. The Skilful Hunter

There once lived a brave hunter. One night, he met three giants in the forest. He told them that he had never missed a shot. The giants wanted him to get the princess who lived in a castle outside the forest.

The hunter agreed and went into the castle. Without disturbing anyone, he picked up a sword and returned to the forest. He tricked the giants and chopped off their heads one by one with the sword.

The king heard and proclaimed, "Whoever killed the giants will marry my daughter!" But the princess did not want to marry just anyone and left the palace. She started living in a hut in the forest.

One day, the hunter was passing by. The princess recognised her father's sword. She realised that the brave hunter had killed the giants and agreed to marry him. The two were soon married and lived happily ever after.

14. The Stork

In a village, a mother stork gave birth to four young ones.

Once, some little boys were playing on the street. They looked up at the stork's nest. Then, they sang rude songs about how the storks would be killed.

The little storks ran to their mother, frightened. Mother Stork told them not to worry, as soon they would learn to fly. Then, they would all fly away to a sunny Egypt. However, all the boys would laugh at the little storks every day. All except a boy named Peter.

As time passed, the storks learned to fly. But before they left, they wanted to take revenge on the boys. Now, we know that storks bring little babies to people. Thus, in anger they took smelly skunks to the rude little boys and a fine little brother for kind Peter.

15. The Peasant

Once, a poor peasant's wooden calf was stolen. He complained to the mayor. The mayor thought it was a real one, and so, gave him a real cow.

The peasant killed the cow and sold its hide. While returning home, it started raining. Thus, he stayed in a miller's house. They played cards all through the night and finally the peasant won three hundred coins.

When the peasant reached home the next day, he told the villagers that he got all the money by selling the hide of one cow. The greedy villagers killed all their cows.

Now, as the truth was revealed, the peasant was given the punishment of drowning. However, he escaped and stole a flock of sheep from a farm. He went back to his village and explained, "There are meadows with plenty of sheep under the water."

Thus, all the villagers jumped into the water and drowned. Now, the peasant was the only person alive!

16. The Juniper Tree

Once, a lady sat under a Juniper tree. She wished for a child as white as snow and red as an apple. Quite soon, she was blessed with a baby boy. However, the poor lady died soon after.

The boy's stepmother disliked him. Thus, she killed him. Then, she cut him up and made a pie of him and fed it to her husband. The boy's stepsister was very sad to see this. She gathered the uneaten bones and buried them under the Juniper tree.

Soon, a bird, sat on the Juniper tree. She started singing about the boy's death. People gifted her a gold chain, red shoes and a mill-stone, to listen to her song.

She dropped the chain on the father and the shoes on the girl. However, she dropped the mill-stone on the stepmother's head and killed her.

Suddenly, the boy came alive. He lived happily with his sister and father, thereafter.

17. Three Little Men

Once, a wicked old woman's ugly daughter and beautiful stepdaughter met three little men in the forest. The stepdaughter greeted them and shared her food. They gave her three boons. She would become more beautiful, gold coins would fall from her mouth and she would become a queen.

The ugly daughter was rude and did not share her bread. The three little men cursed her thrice; she would turn uglier, slimy toads would fall out from her mouth and that she would die painfully.

Soon, the stepdaughter became the queen and lived happily at the palace. However, the old woman and her ugly daughter managed to trick her and threw her into the pond. The daughter then disguised herself as the queen.

The real queen swam in the pond as a duck. One day, she called out to the king and told him about the trickery. The king sentenced the old woman and her ugly daughter to death.

18. Semsi Mountain

Once, there lived two brothers. The elder one was rich but a miser. The younger one was poor but generous.

The younger brother once saw twelve robbers shouting, "Semsi Mountain, Semsi Mountain open up," and a huge mountain opened up. The robbers went inside and came out soon. The younger brother did the same and found a treasure. He picked some money for his family and returned home.

The younger brother used the money to feed his family and help the poor. His jealous brother threatened him to disclose the source of his income. Terrified, the younger brother told him the whole story.

The greedy brother found the treasure and gathered all the wealth in big bags. He then shouted, "Simeli Mountain, Simeli Mountain open up," but nothing happened. In his greed, he had forgotten the mountain's name!

The robbers returned and found him stealing their money. They cut off his head in anger.

19. Brides on Trial

Once, there lived a young shepherd. As he grew up, the shepherd wanted to get married. He knew three sisters in his neighbourhood. They were all pretty. So he found it difficult to choose one as his wife. Confused, he went to his mother for her opinion.

His mother said, "Invite the three sisters for dinner. Serve them cheese and see how each one of them eats it."

The young shepherd invited the sisters. Later, he watched them eat, carefully. The eldest sister gulped the cheese hurriedly without even peeling off the skin. The younger sister peeled the skin carelessly and wasted a lot of cheese. The youngest sister, however, peeled the skin very neatly without wasting a bit and ate the cheese.

The shepherd described this to his mother. The mother asked her son to marry the sensible and patient youngest sister. The shepherd married the youngest sister, happily.

20. The Devil's Sooty Brother

Once, there was a poor soldier called Hans. He met a man in the forest and asked him for food. The man, actually, was the Devil.

The Devil promised Hans great riches if he worked with him for seven years. Hans agreed. He swept the Devil's house and fed his fire with logs of wood. As ordered by the Devil, Hans grew his hair and did not wash his face.

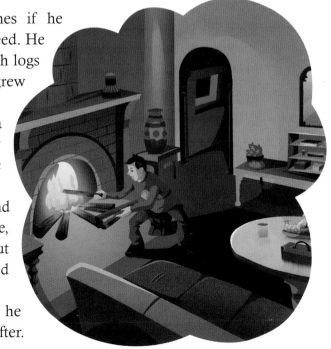

After seven years, the Devil gave Hans a bag of soot and called him the Devil's Sooty brother. However, as Hans watched – the soot in the bag turned into gold.

On his way home, Hans saw an inn and decided to rest. Seeing his untidy appearance, the innkeeper refused to let him enter. But when innkeeper heard that Hans worked with the Devil, he gave him the best room.

Hans continued his journey. Finally, he reached home and lived comfortably thereafter.

21. Godfather Death

A poor man wanted to appoint a godfather for his son. He had refused the offers of God and Devil. Then, he accepted Death as his son's godfather. He believed that Death was fair to the rich and poor.

When the boy grew up, Death gave him the gift of healing people but warned that he could only heal them if Death was at their head. The boy became a doctor and healed many people.

Once, a beautiful princess fell ill, and had Death at her feet. However, the doctor healed her.

Death was very angry now. He said, "I put a new life on earth only when an old life dies. It was the princess' turn to die. Yet you healed her. Now I will take you with me instead of her, to make space for the new life. You should always fulfil your promise!" Thus, Death killed his own godson.

22. The Talented Brothers

Once, there was a king whose daughter had been captured by a fierce dragon. So, he announced that whoever rescues the princess, would marry her.

Now, there were four skilful brothers. One was an astronomer, one a tailor, one a thief and the youngest a hunter. They took up the task.

Using his telescope, the astronomer located the dragon on an island. The brothers set out on a ship. When they reached the island, they found the dragon asleep. Quickly, the thief stole the princess and took her away to the ship. Suddenly, they heard the dragon roaring above them and the hunter shot him. He fell down dead on the ship! Alas! The ship broke. The tailor swiftly sewed back the entire ship.

Safe, they returned to the palace. Now, they started arguing about who would marry the princess. In the end, the king decided to reward them with half his kingdom, and find someone else for his daughter!

23. The Lazy Sons

Once, an old king called his three sons. He announced that his laziest son would inherit his entire kingdom.

The eldest son said, "Father, I should get your kingdom. I am so lazy that if a drop of water falls on my eye I do not care to wipe it."

The middle son said hurriedly, "No father, only I can get your kingdom. I am so lazy that I let my heels burn at the fireplace but do not move back my leg, out of laziness."

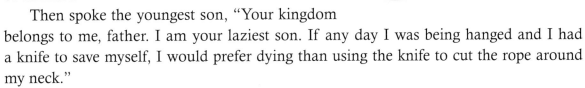

Then spoke the youngest son, "Your kingdom belongs to me, father. I am your laziest son. If any day I was being hanged and I had a knife to save myself, I would prefer dying than using the knife to cut the rope around my neck."

The old king decided that his youngest son was the laziest of all and made him the king.

24. The Donkey Prince

Once there lived a king and a queen. Their son was cursed to looked like a donkey. He loved music and became a very good lute player.

One day, the prince saw his ugly face in a well. He became very sad and left the royal palace. He reached a kingdom where a king lived with his beautiful daughter. The king was very happy to hear the donkey play the lute so well. He was so impressed that he married his daughter to the donkey.

Now, the king hid himself in their room. At night, he saw that the donkey took off his skin and became a handsome prince. When he fell asleep, the king burnt the donkey's skin.

The next morning, the happy king gave his entire kingdom to the handsome prince. Thus, the prince and his wife lived happily forever.

25. The Helpful Frogs

Once, a king had a son, who was a simpleton. The king was worried about the prince's future and sent him away to learn the ways of life. The prince reached the forest and sat near a pond. A frog saw the sad prince and asked him, "What troubles you?"

The prince told the frog his story. The frog took him to the bottom of the pond and introduced him to the other frogs. They all made him a wise human.

Soon, the prince decided to leave for home. The frogs gifted him a female frog. The female frog said, "We have helped you a lot. I want you to kiss me in return."

The kind prince kissed her. Immediately, she turned into a beautiful princess. The prince was very happy and took her to his palace. The king welcomed them both and soon married the prince to the princess.

26. The Devil's Deal

Once, three injured soldiers were lying on the battlefield. There was no one to help them. Suddenly, the Devil stood before them and said, "I will spare your life, if you agree to give me your souls after seven years. But, I will ask you a riddle, if you answer correctly, I'll set you free." The soldiers had to agree!

Now, the Devil took them to a beautiful palace and filled their pockets with gold. The soldiers lived comfortably. Soon, the seven years were about to end. The scared soldiers decided to hide in the forest.

While roaming the forest, the soldiers met an old lady. Now, this lady was the Devil's grandmother. Being kind-hearted, she told them the answer to the riddle. They rushed back to their house. When the Devil came, he asked them the riddle.

As they answered correctly, the Devil flew into a rage and disappeared. And the soldiers were free!

27. The Lucky Boy

Once, there lived a poor couple, who had a baby boy. No one in the village would agree to be his godfather, except for a poor old man.

As a gift, the old man gave the boy's father a key and instructed to give it to him when he grew up. Time flew by. The father gave the boy the key and told him to find a castle by a mountain.

The boy set out in search of the castle and despite many difficulties found it. He opened the door to the castle. A finely dressed old man greeted him with open arms. He was the boy's godfather! He was a rich lord, who had been cursed. The boy had freed him.

Now, the godfather invited all of them to come and live with him in his castle. Thus, the boy and his family spent their days in comfort.

28. A Small Boy's Dream

One night, a small boy dreamed that he had found a golden box. He woke up feeling very happy. It was winter. That day, he went outside to find the golden box. He pulled his cap over his ears and walked on.

Near his house, was a magical forest, full of beautiful trees and whispering sounds! He wished he would meet an elf or the king of trees. Suddenly, his foot struck something hard. He dug in the ground and found a tiny golden box! Then, he saw that something else shone in the mud! Ah, a tiny key! He pushed the key into the hole and opened the box.

Inside, there was light that turned into a beautiful lady. She said, "Little boy, you have released me from a curse. I bless you with happiness always." Then she disappeared.

Her words were true, for the small boy lived happily ever after.

1. The Days of the Week

The Days of the Week were always busy. Thus, they only met every four years, on the 29th day in February for a party.

The days came dressed in carnival clothes. They exchanged stories and poked fun at each other.

Sunday, the leader of the days, came in a black silk gown. Monday, was a young man. He always wanted to enjoy himself, as the week began with him. Tuesday, was a day of strength. He loved helping everyone to prepare for the coming days. Wednesday, was right in the middle, so he marched with three days before him and three after him.

Thursday, was a coppersmith. He always tried to show his power and noble character. Friday, was a free and cheerful young lady. She wanted to find a husband for herself. Saturday, was an old housekeeper. She carried her dusting pan and broom and only had soup.

The days had a merry time all day.

2. The Lucky Tailor

Once, a tailor was travelling alone. He had been warned not to travel at night, but he said, "I am lucky. God always takes care of me."

Night descended and he climbed a tree to be safe from wild animals. Suddenly, he heard loud sounds and saw a stag and a bull, fighting. They shook the tree, so he got down for safety. The stag killed the bull and picked up the frightened tailor in his antlers and ran.

When the stag stopped, he put the tailor down gently. Then, the stag pushed open a rock and said, "Hurry! Come inside quickly."

The surprised tailor followed. There was a huge hall behind the rock! There, lying on the ground was a transparent chest with a miniature castle. In another chest was the loveliest maiden he had ever seen.

The tailor lifted the chest lid and in a flash, the maiden awoke, and the stag turned into a handsome man!

"You've broken the curse," said the maiden, who was actually a princess.

The stag was her brother. A wicked magician, who had turned the brother into a stag, had cursed them. The princess was sent into a deep sleep. The castle and kingdom were shrunk and placed inside a chest. Then one day, the wicked magician had turned himself into a bull. The stag saw his chance and chased him and killed him.

"So, this is what happened to us. I have seen you saving me in my dreams," concluded the princess.

The tailor opened the lid of the second chest and a huge castle sprang up. The kingdom grew until everything became as large and wonderful as it should be.

The beautiful princess and the lucky tailor were married. The handsome brother became the king and everyone lived happily.

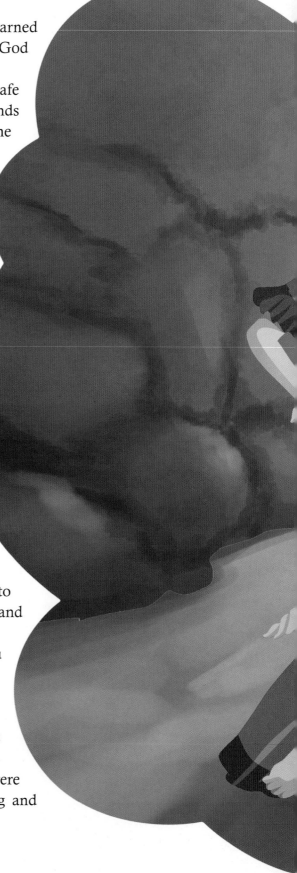

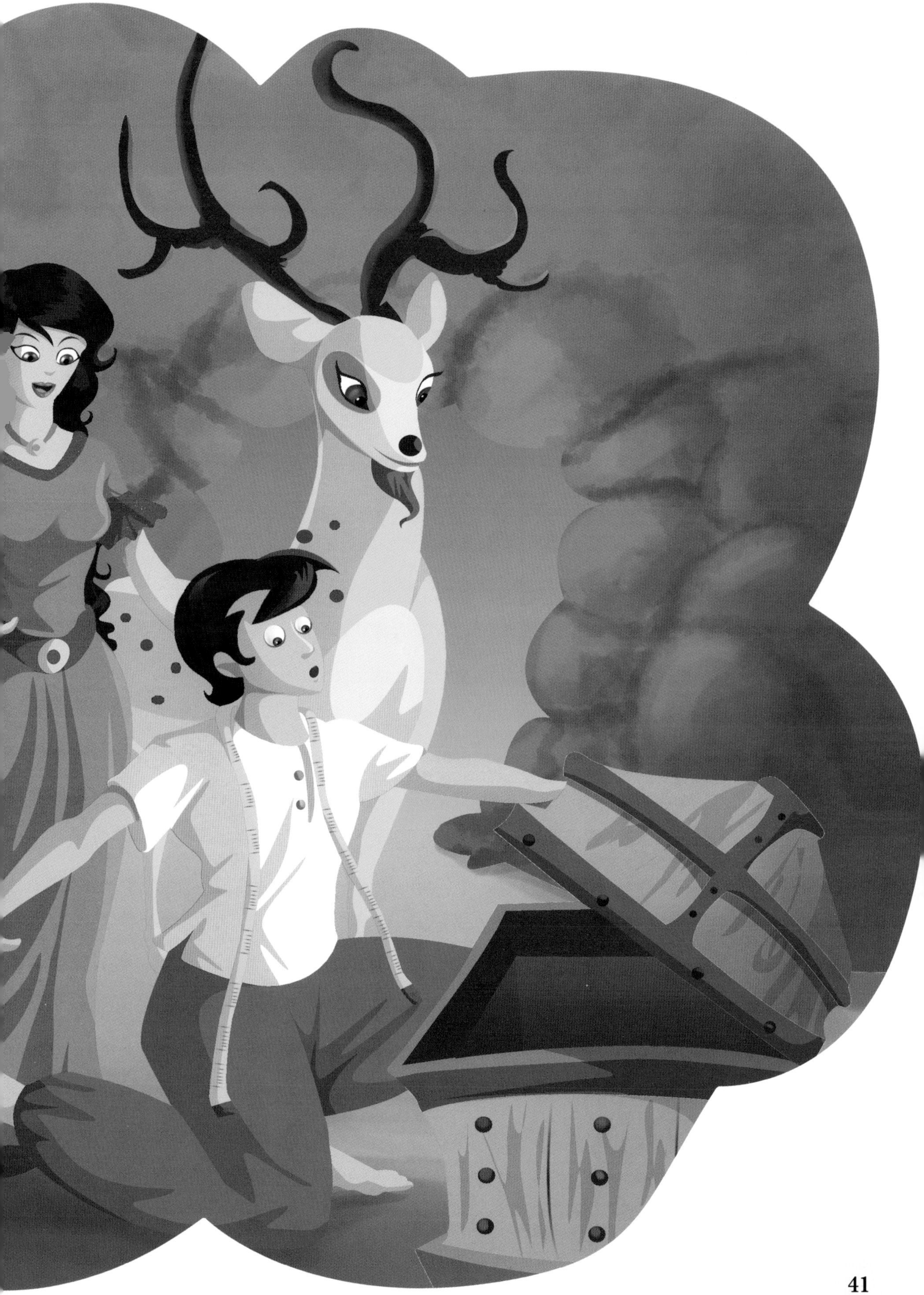

3. The Rich Farmer's Soul

There lived a rich farmer in a village. One day, the farmer helped his poor neighbour with food for his starving children. Then, he said, "When I die, watch over my grave for three nights." The neighbour agreed.

Soon after, the farmer died. The neighbour watched over his grave for two nights. On the third night, a soldier joined him. That same night, the Devil came and said, "Let me take the farmer's soul and I will give you gold in return."

The soldier said, "Fill my boot with gold and we'll leave." The Devil went to get the gold. Meanwhile, the soldier removed the boot sole and placed it over a hole in the ground. Now, when the Devil filled it with gold, it dropped into the hole and the boot remained empty!

At sunrise, the tired Devil ran away. The farmer's soul was saved and the soldier and the neighbour became rich.

4. Three Brothers

Once, a man told his three sons, "Go and learn a craft. I shall leave my house to the one who is best at his craft." Thus, the boys left home to complete this mission.

The eldest son became a blacksmith, the second son a barber and the youngest son a swordsman. They returned home to show their father their skills.

The eldest son changed the shoes of a galloping horse and impressed his father. The second son saw a running hare and shaved off its whiskers, perfectly.

'Let's see what my youngest does,' the confused man thought. Suddenly it started raining. The youngest son moved his sword so fast that not a drop fell on him and he was completely dry. The man gave his house to the youngest son.

All the sons loved one another as true brothers. Thus, they lived together, happily.

5. What the Moon Saw

A poor painter lived in a strange town. He had no friends there and was very sad. However, the moon became his friend. The moon would peep into his window almost every night and describe things that it saw. The painter would then paint what the moon saw.

The first evening, the moon described a beautiful maiden on the banks of a river. The second evening the moon spoke of the innocence of a child. The moon then spoke of situations of death, honour, of loyalty, loss and other things.

One evening, the moon spoke of a little boy. He was a good boy and knew all his prayers well. One night, his mother asked him, "What do you mumble after 'give us this day our daily bread?' "

The boy guiltily replied, "And lots of butter on it." The moon and the painter laughed heartily at that!

6. The Soldier and the King

Once, a hungry soldier and a man were walking through a forest. Soon, they saw a house. In the house, they saw a lady, cooking food. She warned them that the house belonged to robbers and hid them. The robbers came in and looked around. They found the soldier and the man.

The soldier said, "Kill me later. First feed me!"

The surprised robbers gave them food. The soldier, who was also a magician, waved his hands and the robbers froze.

The soldier told the man that he would bring some soldiers from the nearest town. He went and came back with many soldiers. The soldier waved his hands again and the robbers unfroze.

The soldiers tied up the robbers and bowed low before the man. The man was actually the king! The king then said to the soldier, "Eat at my table all your life. Just don't wave your hands at me!"

7. Mrs. Wolf and Mr. Fox

Mrs. Wolf asked Mr. Fox to be her baby's godfather. Mr. Fox agreed and was invited to the feast. Mr. Fox ate well at the feast. Then, he said, "The baby needs something nice to eat."

Mrs. Wolf agreed and they went to the sheepfold. There, the wolf saw the sheep in the pen and crawled in. The fox lay down to rest by the fence.

The shepherds saw the wolf. They beat her and poured hot, washing liquid over her. Limping and scalded, she dragged herself to the fence.

Seeing her, the fox said, "I am also badly beaten. Please pick me up and take me home. Otherwise, I will die."

The poor Mrs. Wolf was aching all over; somehow she brought Mr. Fox home and put him down. The fox jumped up and said, "I am well. You are such a fool! How can a fox be a wolf's godfather?"

Then he ran away, laughing.

8. The Son Who Could Wish for Anything

Once, a queen prayed for a child. An angel appeared before her and said, "You will have a son who will be able to wish for anything!"

The queen had a son, but the cook stole him. The king got angry with the queen. He put her in a dark tower, but God sent two doves to feed her, so, she stayed alive.

Meanwhile, the boy grew up lonely. Once, he wished to meet a beautiful girl. She appeared and they married each other.

Soon, the boy came to know that the cook had stolen him. The furious boy punished him by turning him into a dog.

Now, the boy wanted to see his mother. Thus, he went to meet the king. When the king learned that his son was alive, he brought his queen back. The boy and his mother were reunited. They all lived happily.

9. The Old Man and His Grandson

There was an old man who lived with his son and daughter-in-law and their little son. He was a sweet little boy who loved his grandfather dearly.

The old man would drool while eating, since he had very few teeth left.

One day, seeing his father drool, the son became angry. He made the old man sit behind the stove and gave him a clay bowl to eat in. The old man cried and looked longingly at the good food on the dining table.

After a couple of days, the son saw his own son making a big clay trough. The child saw his father and said, "This is for you and mother. grandfather only needs a bowl. You and mother will need a trough to eat in."

The son realised that he was treating his father badly. He apologised to his father and said, "Father, from now on, we will all eat together at the dining table."

10. The Bear and the Two Travellers

One day, two friends travelled together to see the world. During their journey, they reached a dense forest. The two friends walked close to each other. Suddenly, they heard loud growling sounds behind them.

The bold friend quickly climbed a nearby tree. He sat on the topmost branch and covered himself with leaves. The other friend was unable to climb and found no place to hide. So he lay down on the ground, closed his eyes and pretended to be dead.

Soon, a bear appeared. He smelt the boy on the ground and thought that he was dead. A bear does not eat the dead, so he went away.

A little while later, the first friend climbed down the tree and asked him, "What did the bear whisper in your ear?"

His friend replied, "He said that I should not travel with a friend who leaves me alone in danger!"

11. The Thief and His Father

Once, a man lived in a village with his son. One day, the son stole some sweets. He told his father about the theft; however, his father did not punish him.

Now, the son became confident and stole something or the other every day. After a few years, he was known as the Village Thief and became notorious for big thefts.

One day, the people reported him to the king. The king sent his soldiers to the village to catch the thief. While they were taking the thief to the prison, the father came to meet his son. The son shouted at his father in rage. The father said, "Why are you shouting at me, son?"

He replied, "Parents always stop children from doing wrong things. But, you never stopped me from stealing. You are responsible for me becoming a thief!"

The father realised his fault, but it was too late!

12. Twelve Hunters

Once, a prince met a beautiful girl in a forest and married her. Soon after, the king called him to the palace.

The king was ill and requested his son to marry the princess of the neighbouring kingdom. Since it was his father's last wish, the prince promised to do so.

The king died. The prince announced his engagement with the princess.

When the prince's wife in the forest heard this, she felt betrayed. She called eleven hunters. Then, she disguised herself as the twelfth and went to the palace.

The twelve hunters met the prince. One of them showed him a diamond ring that he had given to his wife. Tears flowed down the prince's eyes as he remembered his wife.

When his wife saw this, she revealed her true identity. The prince was very happy to see her again.

Then, he did not marry the princess and lived with his wife happily ever after.

13. The Jumper

Once, a flea, a grasshopper and a rabbit were having a jumping competition. Everyone was invited. The king of the forest offered his daughter in marriage to whoever jumped the highest.

The flea stepped first. He bowed before everyone and jumped so high that no one could see him. Everyone thought he did not jump at all.

Next was the grasshopper, looking bright and green. He jumped into the king's face. The king thought it was very rude. Both the flea and grasshopper thought they were eligible to marry the princess.

Then came the rabbit. Without saying a word he jumped straight into the lap of the princess.

Then the king said, "The highest leap was taken by him who jumped up to my daughter."

"For this, one needs to have a brain," added the king. Thus, the rabbit married the princess. The flea and the grasshopper went their ways, very disappointed.

14. The Man and St. Peter

Once, a man was travelling alone. Soon, St. Peter joined him, disguised as a beggar. The man shared his food with him. When his money finished, the man prepared to beg with St. Peter.

St. Peter revealed his true form and said, "Whatever you wish for, will appear in your knapsack."

That night, the man was troubled by nine devils. He wished they would enter his knapsack.

The next morning, the man took his knapsack, filled with the nine devils, to the ironsmith. The ironsmith beat it till eight devils died. The ninth ran away to Hell.

Many years later, the man died. He accidentally first went to Hell. The ninth devil, who had escaped, opened the door, recognised him and shut the door tight.

The man wished he were in Heaven. Lo, he appeared in Heaven! St. Peter was surprised by his sudden arrival but welcomed him to stay.

15. The Three Leaves

Once, a youth married a princess. The princess made him promise that he would have to end his life whenever she died.

Unfortunately, very soon, the princess died of an illness. The youth stayed in the room where the princess' body lay. Everybody thought that he would die of hunger.

Suddenly, he saw a snake slither towards the princess' body. The youth hit the snake thrice. Just then, another snake entered the room carrying three leaves. It placed the leaves on the wounds and the dead snake was alive again!

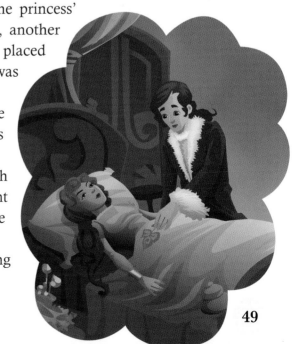

The youth then placed the leaves on the princess' body. She was alive again! He asked his servant to keep the leaves safely.

Sadly, the princess no longer loved the youth and got him killed. However, the youth's servant placed the three snake-leaves on his body. The youth became alive again!

He told the king about the trickery. The king punished the princess.

16. The Drop of Water

There was once a magician called Kribble-Krabble. One day, he looked at a drop of puddle-water with a magnifying glass. He saw tiny creatures struggling with each other. Kribble-Krabble added a drop of a witches' blood to see the creatures more clearly. The creatures became pink in colour.

Kribble-Krabble then asked his friend to look through the magnifying glass. The friend looked and saw a terrible sight. The creatures were actually people, and they were beating each other harshly. The ones on top were being pulled down and the ones at the bottom were struggling to come up.

The friend saw the people catch a lame man and quickly eat him up. A girl was sitting quietly hoping for a piece but the people pulled her too and ate her up. The friend said that the drop seemed to be some huge city like Paris or London.

Kribble-Krabble laughed aloud and said, "Ah! It is a drop of puddle-water!"

17. The Old Street Lamp

Once, in a village lived a street lamp. This lamp was very old and was to retire the next day. It had to be taken to the town-hall and its future was to be decided there.

On its last night, the wind gifted the lamp memory, so that it would never forget anything. The stars gave the lamp the gift to see, clearly, everything that it remembered. If wax lights were put in it, people around the lamp would also see what it thought.

The next day, the village watchman was allowed to keep the street lamp. However, the watchman only oiled the lamp. Thus, he never saw what the lamp remembered.

When the watchman died, the lamp was melted into a candle-stick to hold wax tapers. A poet bought the candle-stick. When the poet started writing, the lamp helped him picture things more beautifully. Thereafter, the two created many beautiful poems.

18. The Shirt-Collar

Once, there was a gentleman who possessed a boot-jack, a hair-brush and a shirt-collar.

Now, the collar wanted to get married. He tried to talk to a garter but she was shy. So the collar lied that he was a fine gentleman who owned a boot-jack and hair-brush but the garter did not give in.

Then the collar spoke the same lies to a glowing-iron and scissors but the glowing-iron burnt his edges and the scissors snipped him badly. He became useless and was thrown away. The hair-brush too turned him down.

One day, the collar was taken to a paper-mill but he lied and boasted there about how he had been loved by a garter, glowing-iron, scissors and hair-brush.

Eventually, the collar was converted into paper as a punishment for having lied to everyone. We must take this as a lesson to be careful about how we act. Telling lies never gets us anything.

19. A Ray of Hope

Once, at the Swedish coast, there was a dark building. Criminals were kept in that building.

One evening, when the sun was setting, a sunbeam entered the cell of one of the prisoners because sun shines upon both, the evil and the good.

The prisoner looked impatiently and angrily at the sunbeam. Then a little bird flew towards the window, for even birds fly to the good and the evil alike.

The bird cried, "Tweet, tweet" and sat near the window. It fluttered its wings, pecked a feather from one wing and then puffed itself out neatly.

The chained prisoner looked gently at the bird. He felt he had some connection with the sunbeam, the bird and the smell of the flowers, which grew under the window of his cell.

Soon, the bird flew away and the sunbeam vanished. Even then, the sunbeam and the bird had touched the heart of the prisoner. He felt sorry for his bad deeds.

20. The Wild Man

In an enchanted forest, lived a wild man who had magical powers.

One day, a prince came to the forest for hunting. To test him, the wild man appeared as an old man and begged him for food. The kind prince gave him some food, as well as some gold coins. Satisfied, the wild man reappeared as himself and told the prince that he would always be there to help him.

The prince liked a princess. However, to marry her, he had to catch the magic apple to be thrown by the princess, during the royal tournament. Thus, the prince went to the wild man who gave him a magic outfit and a horse.

The next day, the prince went to the tournament. None of the other suitors could catch the apple! Finally, the prince caught it and married the princess.

The good wild man helped them all his life.

21. The Three Golden Hair

Once, a boy went to marry a princess. However, the princess said, "I shall marry you, if you fetch the Devil's three golden hair."

Thus, the boy began his journey. Soon, he came across a town. The watchman said, "You can pass after telling me why our fountain of wine has dried up. Also, tell me why our golden apple tree does not bear any fruit now."

The boy said, "I shall tell you when I return!" and he passed the gates. Soon, he reached Hell. The Devil was sleeping. He hid under the Devil's bed.

In his sleep, the Devil said, "There is a frog stuck in the fountain of wine. A rat is eating the roots of the golden apple tree." The boy plucked three golden hairs from his head.

On his way back, the boy answered the watchman's questions. Then, he married the happy princess.

22. The Singing Bone

Once, the king of Whiteville announced, "Whoever will kill the dangerous tiger shall be married to my daughter."

A kind man and a vain man went to the forest to kill the tiger. Quite soon, they saw the dangerous tiger. The kind man killed the tiger with his spear.

The vain man was very jealous of the kind man. Thus, he killed the kind man and buried him in the forest. Then, he married the king's daughter.

After many years, a woodcutter saw a bone lying in the forest. He thought, "I shall gift this to my wife!"

However, when the woodcutter picked up the bone, it began singing, "I killed the tiger, but my friend betrayed me…"

The woodcutter got scared and took it to the king. When the king heard the bone's song, he understood that it was the kind man's bone. The king put the vain man in prison. The vain man was punished for his cruel behaviour.

23. The White Snake

Once, a man touched a white snake. This gave him the gift of understanding the language spoken by birds and animals. With this gift, the man solved the problems of a fish, the King of Ants and a raven. Now the man wanted to marry a princess. She had three conditions.

First, the princess threw her ring into the sea. The man had to find it. The fish, whom the man helped, swam into the depths of the sea and brought out the ring.

Next, the princess spilled sacks of millet grains in the garden. The man was required to collect the grains overnight. The King of Ants helped him. Lastly, the princess asked the man to bring an apple from the tree of life. The raven flew across the seas and brought the apple.

The princess happily married the man! The man understood that one good turn always deserves another.

24. Little Tuk

There was once a boy called little Tuk. He had an examination the next day and had to learn the names of all the towns in Zealand.

However, Tuk's parents left him at home to take care of his little sister, so he could not study. When his mother returned, she told Tuk to go help the old washerwoman carry her clothes.

When little Tuk returned and sat down to study, it became dark and there was no light. Thus, he put his geography book under his pillow and slept.

Tuk dreamt of the washerwoman. She said, "You helped me today. I'll help you learn for your test." Then Tuk dreamt of a hen from Kjoge, a parrot from Presto, a knight from Wordingburg and others from all the towns of Zealand.

When Tuk awoke, he couldn't remember his dream. However, as he revised his lesson, he recalled the names of all the towns in Zealand!

25. The Shadow

Once there was a learned man who lost his shadow. However, he got a new shadow, soon.

After many years, the man's old shadow returned to meet him. The shadow had grown and looked like a man. He invited the man to travel with him. However, the shadow wanted to travel as the master with the man as his shadow. The man agreed and so they travelled.

While travelling, a beautiful princess met the shadow and fell in love with him, thinking he was really a man. The shadow asked the man to behave like a shadow before the princess. The man became angry and threatened to tell the princess the truth. Before he could do anything, the shadow went and told the princess that his 'shadow' had gone insane and should be arrested.

The man was soon thrown into prison. Meanwhile, the shadow and the princess were married. But once she knew it was just a shadow that she married, the princess got angry and expelled him from her palace.

26. The Story of a Mother

One cold winter, a worried mother sat by her sick child. An old man came to her house to rest. The man was Death.

The mother closed her eyes for a moment to rest but when she woke up, she saw that Death had taken her child away. The mother asked people to help her find Death's house. When she reached, Death had not yet arrived, so she waited.

When Death arrived, the mother begged Death to return her baby. Then Death asked her to look into a well. She saw the future of two children, one whose life was filled with joy and the other's filled with misery. Death told her that one of them was her baby's future.

The mother fell on her knees and prayed to God to take the decision he had made, for it would be for the best. Then, Death carried her baby away. This time the mother did not cry.

27. The Buckwheat

Often, after a very violent storm the field becomes full of buckwheat. Buckwheat is an edible seed and looks as if it were burnt. The old willow tree relates the story of the Buckwheat.

Being very old, the old willow tree had grass growing out of it. Now, there was a field of buckwheat growing opposite the tree. The buckwheat was very proud and would stand straight all day.

When the storm came, all the flowers and plants of the field bowed their heads till the storm passed over. Everyone but the buckwheat! The old willow begged the buckwheat to bow down, but it refused.

After the storm, the willow cried out. When they asked him why, he pointed out to the buckwheat. It lay on the ground like a burnt weed. The lightning had destroyed it and the old willow cried for the buckwheat's foolishness and how he suffered for it. Till today the seeds of buckwheat carry the burnt marks.

28. The Shepherd

A prince from a small kingdom wanted to marry the emperor's daughter.

On the prince's father's grave, grew a rose bush with the most beautiful roses. A nightingale sat there, and sang delightfully. The prince sent the roses and the nightingale to the princess but she rejected them.

Then, the prince dressed as a shepherd and made a pot that could tell what every stove was cooking. He gave it to the princess in return for ten kisses. Next, he made a rattle that played every tune there was on earth. However, he was only willing to exchange the rattle in return for a hundred kisses. The princess took that as well.

When the emperor saw the princess with the shepherd, he banished her from the kingdom.

The prince then revealed himself. He was very upset that the princess had rejected precious gifts from a prince, but paid in kisses for simple toys from a shepherd. He also left her and went back to his kingdom.

29. The Top and the Ball

A top and a ball were placed together in the same box. The top asked the ball to marry him. The ball, quite pretty in fine leather dress, refused. She told the top that she was already half engaged to the swallow.

One day, a little boy was playing with the ball. She bounced very high and never came back. The top thought that she had gone to live with the swallow.

Years went by and the top still thought of the ball. Although he was old, he was still golden and shiny.

One day, the top spun so fast that he landed in the dustbin. Among all the garbage, he saw the ball. She was old and shabby. She told him that she fell into the gutter and was there all this while.

The garbage-man then came to clean up the dustbin. He picked up the shiny top and left the ball behind.

30. The Farmer's Wife

Once, a farmer and his wife lived in a village. They were generous and helped everyone.

God was so happy with them that He blessed them with a special son. God promised the farmer's wife in her dream that He would take care of the baby.

Soon, the wife gave birth to a baby boy. One day, the wife took him to watch a circus. Suddenly, a lion broke his cage and ran out. The wife and her son got separated in the chaos.

She closed her eyes and cried aloud, "God took my son away. I will not pray to him."

However, when she opened her eyes, her son was standing before her.

He said, "I was lost but an angel led me to you. He said God had sent him to help me."

The wife's eyes filled with tears of happiness. She realised her mistake and thanked God.

31. The Wicked Prince

There once lived a wicked prince. All he did was conquer countries, frighten people and cause trouble.

Now, the prince had become so full of his victories that he thought, "I am the greatest person and no one is more powerful than me. I can conquer even God." Thus, he ordered his carpenters to construct a powerful ship that would rise above the skies.

Soon, the ship was ready. When it was in the air, God sent an angel to stop it. The wicked prince sent many bullets flying towards the angel. However, nothing happened. The angel shed just one drop of blood, which burnt the entire ship and it went crashing to the ground.

Then, the prince built a better ship. This time God sent gnats. One little gnat got into the prince's clothes and stung him. The wicked prince cried out in pain – he had learned his lesson well!

1. The Giant and the Tailor

An old legend had it that the country forest was home to a fierce giant, who feared God.

One day, a tailor wandered into the forest. As he was walking, he saw a tall tower at a distance. The curious tailor went close, but it turned out to be the god-fearing giant!

The giant shouted, "I will eat you, human!"

"Don't eat me! I will work for you," the scared tailor said. The giant asked him to fetch water. "I will bring the river!" said the tailor.

The giant was frightened and said, "Oh no! That will anger the God of Water!"

Then, the giant asked for three boars. The clever tailor laughed, "I will give you a thousand boars."

The giant said, "No! The God of Animals will get angry."

Too frightened to ask for anything else, the giant let the tailor return home.

2. The Nail

A merchant had travelled to a village fair and sold all his goods. Pleased with his fortune, he heaved bags of silver and gold over his horse and set off. He was in a hurry to reach home by nightfall. He rode as quickly as he could. By afternoon, he felt hungry and the horse needed hay and water.

The merchant stopped at an inn for his night meal. He told the stable boy to feed his horse. The stable boy looked at his horse and said, "Sir, your horse's shoe is loose, because a nail is missing. There is a blacksmith close by. Shall I call him?"

"No," said the merchant, who had quickly eaten his food. "One missing nail, one loose shoe won't matter. I have to go now."

The horse trotted smartly, but gradually slowed down. The merchant whipped him, but the horse started stumbling. Finally, he got off the horse to lessen the weight, but the horse still limped. After a short distance, the horse fell and his loosened shoe fell off. He got up and limped away to eat grass by the wayside.

"Oh God," groaned the merchant. "This is all my fault. I should have called the blacksmith and got the nail fixed. So much delay because of my hurry! I will never reach home tonight! I will have to leave my money unguarded if I go to get some help. Oh, what if someone steals it?"

He thought for a while as to what he could do. Then, he tied his horse to a tree. He covered his bags of gold and silver coins with branches and grass. He started to walk back to the inn to fetch the blacksmith, and pledged never to ignore small but important things in haste.

3. The Wolf and the Fox

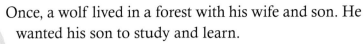

Once, a wolf lived in a forest with his wife and son. He wanted his son to study and learn.

So, the wife asked the fox to teach her son every evening. The cunning fox visited the wolf's house every evening and stayed till night. Then, he ate their supper and left without teaching the child anything. This continued for many days.

One day, the fox said to the wolf, "Dear friend, we must feed the child with tastier food to sharpen his brain."

The poor wolf agreed and went with him to a farm. The fox told him to go inside and steal food, while he would guard the door.

The wolf went inside to steal a chicken. However, the peasants heard him and beat him. The wolf escaped with difficulty and saw the fox sleeping outside.

Now, he understood the fox's plan and never spoke to him again.

4. The Court Cards

William was a little boy with a huge paper castle. The castle had a drawing room with a court of cards. The pack of Hearts, Diamonds, Clubs and Spades hung in frames from the walls.

One day, William was looking at the cards. Suddenly, the Knave of Hearts jumped out of the frame. He asked William to light a candle. The Knave spoke of the King of Hearts, their ruler; how he would be so pleased with the candle.

The Knave of Diamonds and the Knave of Clubs came next. They brought an axe each for William. He lit candles for them, too. The Knave of Spades, despite being the poorest, came too. William being good-hearted lit four candles for him.

The grateful king and queen danced among the flames. The whole place was lit up like a carnival and everyone had a good time.

5. The Turnip

There once lived a rich brother and a poor brother. The poor brother was a turnip farmer. Once, there grew a gigantic turnip in his farm. He gifted the wonderful turnip to the king. The king gave him a lot of wealth.

The rich brother heard about his poor brother's fate. Out of greed, he took many expensive presents for the king. The king gave him the huge turnip in return. He took the turnip helplessly but was jealous of his brother.

Back home, he decided to kill his brother. He trapped him in a sack. Just then, the poor brother screamed, "I have found the sack of wisdom!"

Hearing this, the rich brother himself got into the sack to gain wisdom. However, he found it empty. He realised his mistake and promised that he would never be jealous of anyone. The poor brother forgave him and they lived happily and peacefully.

6. The Son's Fortune

Once, a man lived with his three sons. Before dying, he distributed his possessions among his sons. The first son got a cow, the second got a horse and the third son got a cock.

The elder sons laughed at the third son and said, "You have inherited such a useless thing."

He replied, "God never creates useless things. You should just know how to use them wisely."

Thereafter, he left home and wandered in many places to use the cock and earn money.

Finally, he reached an island where people had never seen cocks and did not know how to read time. The third son showed the cock and explained, "This creature will call at every hour, and tell you when it is dawn and night."

The king of that island was very pleased with the new discovery! He bought the cock and gave the third son a big fortune.

7. The Well

One day, a little boy and his sister went for a picnic. They played for a while and then sat down to eat. Their mother had packed two apples, two biscuits but only one chocolate. They ate the apples and the biscuits, but fought over the chocolate.

The fight grew long and they both fell in a well. It was very dark and they started crying. The frightened children folded their hands and prayed, "Dear God, please take us out of this well."

Immediately, all the darkness disappeared. They saw a locked door. A voice came out of the door and said, "I will let you go if you throw away the chocolate because of which you were fighting."

The boy and his sister threw the chocolate. Soon, the door opened to a staircase. They climbed it and got out of the well. Now, they decided never to fight again.

8. Lucky Tom

In the garret of an old fashioned house, was born a boy. He was named Tom.

Tom lived in poverty with his parents and grandmother. Grandmother believed that Tom was a special child. Tom was growing to be a good and affectionate boy.

However, one day, war broke out. Tom's father joined the battle. He was killed on the front. It was a great loss for the family. Tom's mother started working.

One day, in the street, Tom saw some boys poking around the gutter. The boys were looking for anything that was lost or hidden. They found only buttons or copper coins.

However, when Tom joined these boys, he found a silver coin. The next day, Tom found a gold ring. He always found something valuable. Therefore, the boys called him Lucky Tom.

Soon, Tom collected a lot of things and helped his mother to get food for them. His grandmother was right – Tom certainly was special!

9. Peter Learns Ballet

Once, a boy called Peter had a godfather who joined the theatre. Peter often went to watch the dress rehearsals at the theatre. He enjoyed the ballet and sang and enacted the scenes at home. Finally, Peter decided to join a ballet class.

One day, Peter met his mother's dear friend, Miss Frandsen, who was once famous in the theatre. She warned him that the theatre could be a tough place. But Peter was not discouraged. He joined a dancing school. He worked hard under the dance master.

Peter soon got the part of a prince in a show. His proud family came to watch. However, as Peter was dancing, his old dress ripped down the back. All the children laughed and called him Ripperip. Still, Peter did not stop dancing.

Peter was a quick learner and did well in his studies, too. Everyone agreed that this was because Peter knew that it was all right to fail sometimes, and hard work never goes waste.

10. The Good-luck Swan

One fine day, three friends – Sunshine, Rain and Wind – met over a mountain. Sunshine began telling her friends the tale of the golden swan that flew over the countryside. The swan was a sign of good luck.

One day, a woman was gathering wood in the forest. She saw the golden swan. It flew away leaving behind a golden egg. She took the egg home and looked after it. The egg hatched, and out came a little swan, which soon flew away. In the egg, she found four gold rings, which she gave to her children.

The eldest child became brave and left home for adventure. He found golden fleece. The other child became a skilled painter and the third a famous composer. The youngest child thought to be a failure, became a well-known poet. Thus ended the story of the swan that brought fortune to the family.

11. The Comet

People in a little village were greatly excited. They were gathering in the streets. The reason for the uproar was a comet.

The comet had been seen in the sky, a huge sparkling star with a shining tail.

A mother sat with her little boy quietly through all the noise. She saw the shadows cast by the candle. She believed in omens and thought her son would soon die. She felt that the comet was a bad omen for her son.

But her son played happily with colourful soap bubbles! The boy did not know his mother's thoughts. He saw his future in the bright soap bubbles. The comet came and he quickly ran out to watch it as it streaked by, before his mother could stop him.

Sixty years later, the boy was an old man. He had lived a healthy and happy life. The comet was to appear again today. He was eager to see the comet and also show it to his grandson! He knew that one should not believe in superstitions.

12. Sam, the Singer

Sam was a little boy with a beautiful voice. He sang all day long. One could hear him sing hymns, jolly songs or ballads. Sam's family always knew when he was home. The house echoed with his singing.

One day, Sam went to see the chapel master. He wanted to become a trained singer. The chapel master asked Sam to sing a song. Sam's beautiful voice flowed throughout the church. The singing master heard the little boy, too. He readily agreed to train Sam.

Sam went home happily. He began practising for longer hours. The master was pleased with his progress.

One day, Sam's voice sounded strange. The master said Sam's voice was changing. Sam was not to sing for at least two years. So he started writing his own music, with notes and words. He waited patiently, and after two years his voice matured. Sam now became a famous singer.

13. The Boarding House

A boy called Jack was to attend a boarding school, far away from home. He went to his boarding school in the train. Herr Gabriel, the owner of the boarding house came to receive Jack.

Along with Herr Gabriel came his five little children and two other boys, Madsen and Primus. The children were falling over each other in their excitement. The other boarders smiled at Jack.

Madame Gabriel welcomed Jack on reaching the house. They ate stuffed turkey for dinner. Jack ate his meal happily and went to his room.

Jack's room looked out into the garden. Through the window, he saw Herr Gabriel come up to the closed window and stick his tongue out. Jack realised that Herr Gabriel was actually looking at his reflection in the windowpanes. Jack had a hearty laugh. He felt the boarding house was not a bad place after all – as the people there were kind and… sometimes funny!

14. Passion for Theatre

Daniel was a young man who had a passion for the theatre. He was a student, living in his tutor's house. Daniel's tutor wanted him to focus on his studies. He told him to keep away from theatre.

The people of the town enjoyed performing in plays. They had their own drama society. The town's doctor was the manager of the society. He was planning a play of Romeo and Juliet for the people. The doctor was keen that Daniel should play Romeo. The doctor's beautiful daughter was Juliet.

The doctor knew the Tutor would never allow Daniel to be a part of the play. He gave the tutor's wife a role in the play. Thus, she told her husband that Daniel could study as well as perform in plays, because it was a good thing that he could act well.

The group performed before everyone. Daniel's acting received loud applause. The tutor agreed that performing in plays was not a bad thing after all!

15. Meg's House

Meg lived in a house where long ago, stood a grand manor. It had been the house of a knight. It had towers and a metal plate with 'Grubbe' engraved on it. This was the family name of the knight.

Now the house had a dwelling built specially for the poultry. Meg was hired to look after them. The butler of the house knew all about the Grubbe family. He told Meg about them.

The knight had a little daughter. He was very fond of her. He took her along when he went hunting. The daughter enjoyed these rides. One day, she went out riding and never returned. Since then, the manor house stood empty.

Little did anybody know that Meg belonged to the same Grubbe family. Meg was the granddaughter of the lost girl. Now, she was back in her home. The crows alone knew and circled Meg's house, cawing the news.

16. The Two Rags

The paper mill had millions of rags stacked around it. The rags were from far and wide, with many tales to tell. A rag from Norway and one from Denmark exchanged stories.

The rag from Norway was proud of their way of life. Norway being a famous mountain country, he spoke of his strength. He believed in the rough life. He said their land had many springs and wells.

It was the turn of the Danish rag to speak. He talked of their rich literature. He praised the charming people, with their pretty smiles. The Danes were honest and never jealous of others. They were patient and had good values.

The wind blew the rags apart. Both were made into paper. A Norwegian boy wrote a love letter to a Danish girl on the Norwegian paper. A poet wrote a poem on the beauty of Norway on the Danish paper. What a wonderful coincidence!

17. The Thistle

A garden with beautiful flowers was the pride of a manor house. Outside this garden, near the fence, grew a thistle bush. The thistle bloomed with flowers despite its thorns.

One day, a group of young men and women came to the house. They walked in the garden admiring the flowers. The girls plucked flowers and gave them to the young men.

One girl wandered alone, looking around the garden. She was from Scotland. Suddenly, she saw the thistle near the fence. The thistle was the flower of Scotland. She eagerly asked the young man of the house to bring her a flower.

The young man plucked a flower from the thistle, despite the thorns pricking his fingers. He gave the flower to the girl. She put it in his buttonhole. The two fell in love. It was indeed a proud day for the thistle, who had brought the two together!

18. Catch an Idea

A young man was deeply interested in poetry. He tried to write, but failed every time. He was looking for ideas. Then, he decided to take help from a wise woman. The wise woman lived in a small house with a beehive by the gate. The garden had a potato field, but no trees or flowers.

On seeing her house, the young man felt that it had no poetry. But the wise woman told the young man, it was the thought that mattered. She believed one could catch an idea anywhere.

Hearing her speak, the young man felt inspired. He began to draw ideas from the potatoes in the field. He wanted to write about the history of the potato. Seeing the beehive, he sketched a story on the hard-working bees.

The wise woman's advice helped the young man realise what one can invent, if one catches hold of the idea.

19. Great Grandfather

Grandfather was loved by the entire family. He became great grandfather when Fredrick, his oldest grandchild had a baby. Fredrick was very close to his grandfather. They talked about many things, fighting and laughing over matters.

Grandfather told many stories of the past. He always felt that the old times were the best times.

One day, Fredrick had to leave for America on family business. His wife and child went too. Fredrick promised to write letters and send telegrams. On reaching America, Fredrick sent a telegram. Grandfather was overjoyed.

After a month, Fredrick was to return. The family was eager to see them. One day, they heard a rumour. The ship bringing Fredrick and his family home was believed to have sunk. The family was worried.

Thankfully, they soon received a telegram from Fredrick, saying they were safe. Great grandfather happily agreed that the present times were good, too!

20. The Two Candles

A wax candle and a tallow candle lived in a manor. The tallow candle was envious of the wax candle. He wanted to be present at parties, enjoying the society like the wax candle.

One day, there was a ball at the house. The wax candle was bursting with pride. Meanwhile, the lady of the house prepared a basket. She filled it with potatoes, apples and the tallow candle.

The basket was for a poor widow and her three children. It was sent with a little boy. The candle was for the boy's mother. She worked late into the night to take care of her family. The tallow candle was sad as it was going to a poor family.

The family was overjoyed, when they received the basket. The mother made hot baked potatoes. They all ate a grateful meal. The tallow candle was now glad to help people become happy, instead of attending the parties of rich people.

21. The Most Incredible Thing

In a kingdom far away, the king wanted to find a groom for his daughter. He thought of a plan. The king started looking for a man who could do the most incredible thing. The reward was the princess and half his kingdom.

One fine day, a competition was held to decide the winner. The men had to appear before a jury. The jury was made up of children and men of all ages.

There were many marvellous things to be seen. However, all agreed that a clock was the most incredible thing. A young man had made it. The beautiful case was built inside out.

Every hour on the clock was represented by an act. One saw Moses, the Garden of Eden and the Three kings with each passing hour. The clock was truly unique. The young man won the most incredible thing – the love of the princess.

22. The Kind Soldier

Long ago, a great battle had been fought in the Danish country. The Danes had won the battle against the enemy. However, it was at a huge cost, as many lives had been lost.

The dead bodies and the wounded lay helpless on the battlefield.

A soldier was walking through the battlefield. Just then, he saw an enemy soldier lying on the ground. The wounded man had been shot in both his legs and could not walk.

The wounded man asked for water. The soldier, being kind, readily agreed. When the soldier went to give the bottle of water, the wounded man shot at him. However, the wounded man was weak and collapsed while shooting. Thus, he missed the shot and the soldier was saved.

Despite the incident, the soldier gave the wounded man water to drink. When the king heard the story, he honoured the soldier for his compassion.

23. The Bride and the Groom

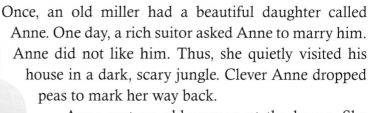

Once, an old miller had a beautiful daughter called Anne. One day, a rich suitor asked Anne to marry him. Anne did not like him. Thus, she quietly visited his house in a dark, scary jungle. Clever Anne dropped peas to mark her way back.

Anne met an old woman at the house. She said, "Go away! This is a murderer's den. He will cut you up and eat you!"

At night, the suitor and his friends came home with a girl. Anne immediately hid in a corner. The men cut the girl into pieces. The suitor chopped the girl's finger to get her gold ring. However, the ring fell beside Anne.

When the men slept, Anne, with the old lady, traced the peas and returned home. The next day, Anne narrated the story before all and showed the girl's ring as proof. The suitor and his friends were at once arrested and executed.

24. The Dwarf Party

Once there lived many big lizards on a tree, deep in the forest. In the same forest, lived many dwarfs. One full moon night, the lizards heard a lot of noise and there was much activity. As the night fell, the lizards watched what the dwarfs were up to.

An open space in the forest was arranged for a grand party. Special guests were invited by the Night-Raven. The dwarf maiden, who was the housekeeper, was busy organising things.

The dwarf king had invited many guests for the party. However, everybody had to come dressed as someone else. Some dwarfs came as animals and the others as birds. Everybody looked wonderful in their colourful dresses. The dwarf dressed as a peacock started dancing with the one that was dressed as a lion. They looked so funny that everyone started laughing loudly!

Gradually, everyone joined in the dance. They were happy to dance and enjoy, leaving aside their worries. Looking at them, the lizards began to dance as well!

25. Ragnard Bolt

Once, a grandson and his grandfather were sitting together. Grandfather was a carver. He had just finished carving the image of Ragnard Bolt with the court of arms. And so, he told his grandson the story of Ragnard Bolt.

Ragnard Bolt dreamt while he slept in a dark cellar of an old castle in Denmark. His long beard had taken root in the marble table upon which he rested. He was a strong soldier of Denmark. Ragnard dreamt of all the good events that would happen in Denmark.

Every Christmas, an angel would visit Ragnard in his dreams. He would confirm that what Ragnard dreamt had actually taken place in Denmark. When Ragnard heard this, he would continue to sleep in peace. Only if Denmark were in danger, he would wake up and strike!

By then, the grandson had fallen asleep and was dreaming of the brave and courageous Ragnard Bolt!

26. Lazy Harry

Harry was very lazy and loved to sleep. He had a goat, but was tired of looking after it. Thus, he married Trina, who also owned a goat. He thought that she would work, while he rested.

Trina, however, was equally lazy. She exchanged both the goats for a beehive. They slept and rested, while the bees busily worked. Soon, they collected a jug of honey.

Harry said, "Trina, you will eat the honey, and it will get finished. Rather, exchange the honey for a goose."

Trina said, "I will keep a goose when we have a son. He will look after it."

"He won't listen to you. Children usually don't listen to parents."

"If he doesn't, I will beat him," said Trina, and picked up a stick and waved it… accidentally breaking the honey jar.

The couple sorrowfully looked at the broken jar and the lost honey. They realised that laziness never does any good!

27. The Philosopher's Stone

A 'Tree of the Sun' grew in a forest. There was a crystal castle on its branches, where a wise man lived. He had a 'Book of Truth,' containing answers to everything.

However, nothing regarding 'Life after Death' was clear to him; thus, he was sad. He had four sons and one daughter, who were blind. He told them about the true, the beautiful, and the good, combined as 'The Philosopher's Stone.'

The eldest brother with a sense of sight; the second brother with a sense of hearing; the third brother with a sense of smell; and the youngest with that of taste, searched for the stone, but in vain. The blind daughter, then, went to look for it with her faith and determination. She discovered that the stone was not a diamond, but the Earth. Just then, they saw the word 'believe' written on the page of the 'Book of Truth.' And they got their eyesight back!

28. Delaying Is Not Forgetting

Once, there was an old mansion where a woman called Mrs. Meta Mogen lived. One evening, some robbers attacked the mansion and killed the servants. Then the robbers tied Mrs. Mogen to the kennel by the chain like a dog, while they themselves went inside the house to eat and rest.

Meanwhile, one of the robbers secretly went to Mrs. Mogen. He reminded her that many years ago, his father had been punished to ride a wooden horse till his legs were paralysed. Right then, Mrs. Mogen had secretly placed pebbles under his feet to help him. The robber wanted to thank her by saving her life. He quietly pulled two horses from the stable and they both escaped.

Mrs. Mogen exclaimed, "Thus the small service done to the old man is being rewarded!"

The robber replied, "Yes! Delaying is not forgetting." He had saved Mrs. Mogen's life!

29. The Windmill

There was once a windmill, which looked very good. It was huge, with four large wings, bright red in colour.

The windmill was owned by a miller, who lived in a house with his wife, close to the windmill. There were also some little boys who would often enter the windmill and run around. The windmill thought of the family as its own.

The windmill thought to itself, "The days are passing and a day will come, when I will be pulled down and built up again. I will become something different, but will live on. My old wood-work and brick-work will rise again."

One day, the windmill caught fire and nothing remained of it, but ashes. The miller's family built a new mill, which was better than the old one. People would look proudly at the new mill. However, the family never forgot its old, faithful windmill.

30. Wonderful Life

Little Mary was the youngest member of the family. On her birthday, she was excited to see her new dress. She got colourful presents and a delicious cake. Mary said it was wonderful to live!

Mary had two older brothers. One was eleven and the other was nine. They loved going to school and playing with their friends. They looked forward to learning new things every day. The boys said they loved life!

Father and mother said, with a smile, "Life is full of surprises! Things do not always happen as we plan!" They agreed that life was a strange, but lovely fairy tale.

Grandfather was an old man but young at heart. He had travelled all over the world. He was always smiling. He told many wonderful stories. Grandfather had seen many things in life, both happy and sad. In all his wisdom, he said life is the loveliest of all fairy tales.

1. The Bell

There was an old mystery in Colourville. Every evening, at sunset, the sweet and peaceful ringing of a bell was heard. However, no one knew where the sound came from.

One day, the prince of Garland decided to go in search of the bell. The prince went to the forest, for the sound seemed to come from there. He walked for a while but could not see the bell.

The tired prince climbed a tree and sat on its highest branch. There, he could see the forest with its green trees and colourful flowers. He could also see the deep blue water of the sea.

"What an enchanting sight!" thought the prince. Suddenly, the bell started ringing. He closed his eyes and listened to it joyfully. He soon left for home, thinking, "I should just enjoy the things I like, instead of questioning what they are and where they are from!"

2. The Emperor's New Suit

Once, there was an emperor who was fond of new clothes. He did not care about his kingdom, and kept himself engaged with his wardrobe.

One day, two cheats came to the emperor's kingdom, saying they were the finest weavers in town. They told the emperor that they could produce the most beautiful dress for him. However, the dress could only be seen by the honest and worthy.

The cheats asked for the finest silk, gold threads and money, to set-up their loom. However, they hid all the cloth and pretended to work on invisible lengths of cloth, using the loom.

After some days, the king asked his senior minister to go and check how beautiful the dress looked. The minister went to the loom, but could see no cloth. Yet, the weavers seemed to be working. They asked the minister if he liked the dress. Speechless, the minister agreed with the weavers, as he did not want to look dishonest and unworthy. He told the emperor that the dress was beautiful. The emperor was very pleased to listen to the description!

Finally, the dress was ready and a procession was organised for the public to see the king's new suit. The weavers pretended to dress the emperor in different pieces of clothes, praising them all the time. However, no one, not even the emperor, could see the dress. They all pretended that they could, for no one wanted to look dishonest.

In the procession, nobody could see the emperor's dress, as there was none. But, no one dared to say, as they feared looking unworthy! However, an innocent child from the crowd said, "The emperor has nothing on him!" It was then that everyone, including the emperor, realised their foolishness!

3. The Old Woman

Once, a little boy's grandfather was telling him a bed-time story, "People say that an old woman lives in the stone castle outside our village. Her back is drooping but her hands are strong. She weaves day and night and never rests. She never leaves the castle but protects all of us from danger."

"How, Grandpa?" asked the boy.

The grandfather said, "Well, she weaves patterns of angels and demons fighting with each other. She can see all future dangers. Thus, she protects us before dangers strike us!"

The boy was amazed. He said, "Oh! I want to go and see the old woman!" His mother said, "The old woman is not real."

However, far away, outside the village, there stood a large stone castle. An old woman, with a drooping back, sat at her loom, weaving. She kept repeating to herself, "I shall save the village from danger!"

4. The Singing Teacher and Harold

Harold was a young man with a great love of music. He had a beautiful voice. He was training with a singing teacher. The singing teacher knew Harold was very talented.

Harold gained a lot of knowledge from his teacher. He loved listening to the stories from the world of music.

Every morning teacher and Harold spent an hour singing. They sang beautiful songs, full of rhythm and expression. The words and melody blended together beautifully. Harold was growing to be a remarkable singer. The teacher was pleased with his progress.

Harold was also developing his acting skills to appear in the theatre. He worked hard, improving on his singing and acting. He was selected to play the lead actor in a musical play.

The singing teacher encouraged Harold. On the day of the play, the teacher earned his reward when Harold's acting and singing skills received thunderous applause and praise.

5. John's First Ball

A small village was buzzing with excitement. The Chief was holding a ball on the coming Saturday. The evening promised dancing and delicious dinner. All the people in the village had been invited.

John and his family were invited too. John was eager to go to his first ball. He enjoyed dancing and listening to music. He was also looking forward to the grand dinner.

Great preparations were made at the Chief's house. The day before the ball, a number of shiny lights hung from the house. John could hardly sleep the night before the ball.

The next day came bright and sunny. The Chief's house stood whitewashed with ivy hanging down its sides. The guests arrived. The men wore tailcoats and the women were in beautiful gowns.

John danced with the Chief's daughter. He enjoyed the grand dinner. John returned home satisfied with the evening.

6. The Elves in the Garden

Hans was a little boy who lived in a house with a beautiful garden. He played with imaginary fairies and elves. Hans made friends with the bees and other insects who had their homes in the garden.

One day, Hans sat by himself in the moonlit garden. There was a mist hanging in the air. The trees swayed in the gentle breeze. Hans gazed into the distance.

Suddenly, Hans saw tiny green creatures flying near the flower-beds. He cautiously went towards them. He hid behind a tree and watched. The tiny creatures were elves. They were talking among themselves. The elves were waiting for their friends. Hans was excited, but stood quietly.

Once all the elves had arrived, a party began. There was singing, chatting and laughing. Soon, they danced in the moonlight. When it was midnight, all of them disappeared. Hans went to bed, dreaming of the dancing elves.

7. Grandmother's Surprise

Edward was a little boy who lived with his parents. He dearly loved his grandmother. She told him wonderful stories and baked cakes for him. However, Edward's grandmother lived in a far away town. He visited her only in summer, during his vacations.

Edward's fifth birthday was near. He wanted his grandmother to be there, too. Although grandmother was scared of trains, she wanted to surprise Edward on his birthday. Despite her fears, she decided to take the train.

Early, the next day, grandmother boarded the train. In grandmother's carriage were a man and his daughter. They could see that she was uncomfortable. The man was a doctor and he began talking to grandmother. They had an interesting conversation. Grandmother did not realise how the time flew by.

Grandmother got off at the station. She went to Edward's house and was greeted by her overjoyed grandson. He loved his grandmother's surprise visit!

8. Laugh and Play

One Christmas, pretty little Dulcie was sitting in her room trying to write poetry. Her brother Harold came bouncing into the room, asking her to stop her foolish poetry and come outside to play a game of soldiers. As much as Dulcie wanted to go, she was offended with his remark, and refused to go with him.

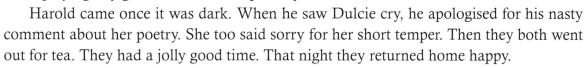

Harold played merrily with his friends, building snowmen, shouting and laughing. Dulcie grew really sad. She missed playing with her brother, as she too loved playing boy games. She sobbed pitifully.

Harold came once it was dark. When he saw Dulcie cry, he apologised for his nasty comment about her poetry. She too said sorry for her short temper. Then they both went out for tea. They had a jolly good time. That night they returned home happy.

So, little boys, when you hurt your sisters, always say sorry!

9. The Elder Tree

Sydney loved to work on his water-wheel sitting near the stream. He did not like to be disturbed. So, when he saw little Walter coming, he told him a frightful story about a ghost in the nearby elder tree, so that he might go away. Scared, Walter rushed back, and played with Madge in the garden.

Later that night, Madge found her necklace missing. Walter went looking for it in the garden. He spotted it near the elder tree, but was terrified that a ghost might attack him if he went nearer. He hurriedly picked the necklace and ran back to the house. However, his foot struck a stone and he fell down.

When Sydney realised that Walter was hurt, he felt guilty about frightening him with the story about the tree. That day, he learned a lesson for life – to always be kind and gentle to those weaker than oneself.

10. The Dale Farm

Dorothy and Oliver's parents had sent them to stay at the Dale Farm with a nurse, while they were abroad. The children were elated to be at the farm.

Every morning they would wake up with the crowing of the cock. Then they watched as Mrs. Farmer fed the geese, turkeys, ducks and hens! They went to the stables and teased the drowsy donkeys.

Then, Dorothy and Oliver rode the horse on the soft ground, covered with thistle and grass. In the afternoon, they sat eating sandwiches in the warm sun, and watched little animals play beside them. They had so much fun!

Soon, it was time to return home. Though they were happy to be home after such a long time, the children were sad to leave their new friends at the farm.

However, they both had been such good children that their parents decided to send them again next year!

11. The Sparrow

Once, an old couple lived on the outskirts of the city, near the forest. The old man was kind and gentle, but his wife was rude and greedy. He loved little birds. He even had a sparrow as his pet, whose melodious songs he loved.

One day, the old man went to the forest to fetch some wood while the sparrow was playing in the garden. It mistakenly pecked at the old woman's grains drying outside. The old woman was angry, and cut off the sparrow's tongue. The sparrow flew away in agony.

The old man was sad to find his sparrow missing, and set out to look for it. Now, the sparrow had magically turned into an angel by then. She welcomed him with gifts for his generosity and love.

The old woman had followed him. She also wanted gifts. However, the Goblins protecting the sparrow, punished her for her misdeeds.

12. The Nightingale

Once, an emperor had a pet nightingale. The nightingale sang the most beautiful and sweet songs that touched everyone's heart. However, the nightingale was not happy, even though she lived in luxury and comfort. For, she no longer had the freedom to chirp and sing in her beloved Greenwood Forest!

One day, a king sent a silver nightingale for the emperor. This bird also sang beautiful songs. The emperor was so enchanted to see her, that he released the old nightingale in the closeby forest.

However, the silver nightingale did not live long and died soon after. Five years later, the emperor was on his deathbed. He longed to hear the nightingale's songs.

The faithful nightingale came to know about the emperor's misery. She flew to his room and sang the most beautiful song ever! The song healed the emperor. He thanked the nightingale and she promised to continue visiting him.

13. The Magpie's Nest

One day, all the birds of the sky went to the magpie to learn how to make a nest, since she made beautiful and the best nests amongst them all. The hardworking magpie, readily agreed to teach them.

She first made a mud cake kind of thing, and said, "This is how thrushes make their nests." Then, she outlined it with twigs. "This is how blackbirds make their nests," she said.

Then, the magpie added some more twigs along the outside, and said, "That is how sparrows make their nests." Then the magpie took some feathers and put them inside the nest. She said, "This is how starlings make their nest."

However, all the birds had flown away by then. They were not good students, and felt impatient with the magpie. When the magpie saw this, she got angry. She decided never to teach them again. And to this day, the magpies make the best nests.

14. How the Wren became the King

Long ago, all the birds of the forest came together to choose the King of Birds.

Everybody was deep in thought when the rooster suggested, "Let's have a competition. First, we will test who flies the highest."

The lark flew high, but the eagle flew the highest. A tiny little bird with no name flew still higher and won the competition.

Then, in the next round, it was decided that the one who dug the deepest hole would be the king. The intelligent little bird hid in a mouse's hole, which went deepest into the earth. Thus, it won this competition, too.

However, the other birds did not want a little bird to be their king. So they asked the owl to guard the mouse hole to stop the little bird from emerging. However, the owl fell asleep, and the little bird escaped. Since then it is known as Hedge-king or wren.

15. The Mistress of the Mansion

Once, there was an old mansion that belonged to a noble family. The mistress of the mansion was very kind and generous.

In the field close to the mansion, there was a little peasant hut. A poor paralysed boy lived there. In the boy's room, towards the north, was a very small window. The boy was unable to walk around and so he would just sit in his room the whole day, looking out through that small window. He could barely see a small piece of the field.

One day, the mistress heard about the boy. The mistress took pity on him and ordered a huge window to be built on the south wall of his room. The boy could now see the forest, the stone castle and the lake. The world had become large and beautiful for the boy, thanks to the kind mistress of the mansion.

16. Tony's Aunt

Tony's aunt was an amusing lady. She was stage-struck. This meant, that she loved theatre and had seen all the plays shown in the theatre close to her house.

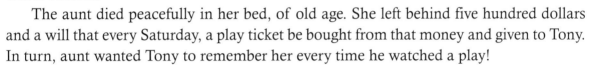

Unfortunately, Tony's aunt had to move out of her house to a new one. This saddened her, because the new house was far from the theatre. Still, she would never miss a play.

Aunt would have been very glad to die in a theatre! Once, she almost did! She was attending a play when the theatre caught fire. In the confusion, she got locked inside and would have burned. Fortunately, the fire was brought under control.

The aunt died peacefully in her bed, of old age. She left behind five hundred dollars and a will that every Saturday, a play ticket be bought from that money and given to Tony. In turn, aunt wanted Tony to remember her every time he watched a play!

17. The Storm Shakes the Shield

When grandpapa was a little boy, people in his town had the custom of hanging shields in front of each building. Each shield was different, and had a sign. Families, and even places, were identified by the shields that hung on their doors.

One night, there was a huge storm. It was so strong that it moved the shields from their original door to another. Thus, when people came out next day to visit places, they landed up at the wrong places because of the wrongly placed shields.

Those who wanted to visit the Institution for Superior Education found themselves at a Billiard Club. Those who wanted to go to a Lecture Assembly reached a noisy Boys' School! People also made mistakes between the church and the theatre. When people realised the storm's confusion, they all had a good laugh!

18. The Toad

In a deep well, there lived a family of toads. The ugliest toad wished to go out of the well. One day, the ugly toad got into a bucket, which was being used by a farmer to draw water from the well.

The farmer, after drawing the water, saw the ugly toad and exclaimed, "Ugh! You are the ugliest thing I have ever seen!" and threw him away.

The ugly toad then travelled and reached a garden where he met a caterpillar. Suddenly, some fowls came to eat the caterpillar but they saw the ugly toad and flew away. The ugly toad became overconfident that his ugliness could achieve anything.

He then decided to travel to the Sun. One day, the ugly toad hopped on a large kite that he thought would carry him to the Sun. As they flew higher, the ugly toad died of heat, crying sorrowfully over his overconfidence.

19. The Nis and Danni

Once, there was a gardener who lived with his wife, Danni. Danni wrote beautiful poetry. But the gardener made fun of his wife's talent.

Now, every day, a magical creature, Nis, would visit Danni's kitchen to eat cream and buns.

One day, the schoolmaster visited Danni. He was very impressed by her thoughts. While Danni sat talking to the schoolmaster about her wish to become a famous poet, Nis heard her.

He even heard Danni saying that she had written a poem about the imaginary creature Nis, titled "The Little Nis."

Nis was so happy that he granted her wish! Lo! In just a few weeks, a publisher came to Danni's house and requested that she give him her collection of poems!

Very soon, Danni became a famous poet and the gardener was sorry that he had made fun of her!

20. The Thief Who Turned into a Bat

Once, there was a thief called Robin.

One day, Robin heard of a rich, old woman, who lived alone. He observed her house carefully and planned to rob her. He felt it would be best to enter the house at night.

At night, Robin entered her house through a window. It was dark and quiet. He switched on the flashlight and started putting the silver and the antiques in his bag. At last, he was ready to leave. Just as he turned, he screamed out. For, the old woman, who was actually a witch, stood right next to him.

Robin tried to run but his legs would not move. He had become still as a statue. The old woman touched his head and muttered something.

Robin sadly realised that because of his wrong habits he had turned into a bat. The old witch laughed heartily as he flew out of the window.

21. The Bond of Friendship

A shepherd lived in a little house in a narrow lane. One day, the shepherd's father came home very late. He also brought a little girl along with him. The girl's name was Anastasia. The Turks had killed her parents, and she was now to be the shepherd's sister.

One day, the bandits killed the shepherd's father. The shepherd was wrongly taken to prison. When he was released, he met a man called Aphtanides. They became friends.

Soon, with the help of his new friend, the shepherd found his sister Anastasia also, and the three started living by the sea.

One day, Anastasia fell into the sea and Aphtanides saved her. The shepherd realised that his dear friend loved Anastasia. Thus, he got the two lovers married. Missing their home, they all returned to the village. Anastasia and Aphtanides lived together happily. The shepherd and Aphtanides stayed friends for the rest of their lives.

22. Not Much

Once, a young man decided to travel. However, he was never content with anything and kept saying, "Not much, not much."

On his way, he met some fishermen. As they took out the net, the young man said, "Not much fish!" The angry fishermen beat him, thinking he was making fun of them.

A little ahead, the king's men were punishing a thief. Again, the young man said, "Not much punishment!" The king's men heard him and yelled, "You must say, may God pity the poor soul."

A while later, he saw a carpenter polishing furniture. The young man said, "Not much polish!" Furious with his words, the carpenter pushed him. The young man collided with a cart full of people, which fell into a pit. The angry driver of the cart thrashed him, too.

The young man went home and decided not to travel without correcting his habit!

23. The Birth of Apes

Once, the Lord and St. Peter visited a city. There they saw a sick and aged beggar. Kind St. Peter requested the Lord to cure him.

The Lord asked a local smith to burn some coal in his furnace. He pushed the old man into the fire. Soon he took the man out and put him in water. As the Lord blessed him, he turned into a young and healthy man. The smith watched all this carefully.

When the Lord had left, the Smith tried the trick on his old mother-in-law. However, unlike the beggar, the old lady screamed in pain.

The smith took her out and put her in water. However, she had become even worse now. The smith's wife and sister-in-law were terrified by the way she looked now. That same night they gave birth to two boys, who were actually apes.

Thus began the race of apes!

24. The Dwarf and the Lady

Once there was a gentle lady. She was very kind and helpful.

One day, she was walking in the forest. Just then, she saw a dwarf in trouble. The end of his beard was stuck in a tree. The lady cut his beard to free him. The ungrateful dwarf, instead of thanking her, called her mean for cutting his beard!

Similarly, the lady helped the dwarf three more times, but he always cursed her.

One evening, the lady saw the dwarf again. He had lots of precious stones. The dwarf saw her and screamed rudely. Just then he heard the loud growling of a bear. The frightened dwarf begged the bear to spare him and eat the lady instead. The bear, however, killed the wicked dwarf at once.

Then, the bear changed into a handsome prince. The dwarf had actually tricked him and taken away his treasure. The lady was happily married to the prince.

25. Frankie and the Dragon

Once, two friends, Frankie and Geordie lived in a village, close to a forest. The boys' parents always warned them, "Don't go to the forest. The dragon will eat you up!"

However, the two friends loved to play in the forest.

One such day, Frankie and Geordie went deep into the forest. It became dark soon. Just then, they heard a growling sound and soon a scary looking dragon appeared.

Frankie at once climbed the closest tree. However, Geordie still stood on the ground and the dragon moved towards him.

Frankie started throwing branches on the dragon and shouted, "Geordie, run!"

The dragon was confused and Geordie started running. Just then, there were loud sounds in the forest. The villagers had come looking for them! The dragon got scared of the noise, and ran away.

Though the boys were scolded for going into the forest, but Frankie was praised for saving his friend's life.

26. The Lost Son

An old man and his wife were sitting outside their house, remembering their son, who got lost while he was little. Suddenly, a handsome, well-dressed Stranger rode up to them.

The old man asked the stranger what he wanted. "A few potatoes the way you eat them, my good man!" he said. The old man asked his wife to prepare a hot potato dish for him.

Then the old man went into the garden to plant saplings. The stranger followed him. He watched the old man tie each sapling firmly to a post. His eyes fell on a crooked tree and he asked, "Did you forget to tie that sapling?"

"Yes. It grew crooked."

"You should have tied me, Father, when I was young," said the Stranger. "I would never have run away and got lost."

The old man and Wife wept tears of joy to find their lost son again.

27. The Drummer

A drummer once found a beautiful handkerchief near a lake. He took it home. At night, a white figure came to him and said, "Give me my handkerchief!"

The drummer gave her the handkerchief. She disappeared saying, "Look for me on the glass mountain."

The next morning, the drummer went searching for the glass mountain. He walked for long, and suddenly, the steep slippery glass mountain rose before him. He wondered how to get to the top.

Just then, he saw two men fighting over a magic saddle. The drummer asked them to race for it. While they went ahead to start running, the drummer sat on it and flew to the mountain top.

There he saw a wicked witch with a beautiful girl. He knocked the witch with the saddle and rescued the girl. The girl was actually a princess. She married the drummer and made him the king!

28. The Clever Thief

Once, there was a clever thief. However, a duke had caught him red-handed. The bold thief said, "You are the only person to catch me!"

The duke said, "I will let you go, if you accomplish two tasks. Bring me my horse, and the sheet I sleep under."

The thief disguised himself as a wine-seller. He went to the duke's stables and distributed free drinks. Soon, the grooms fell asleep and he led the horse straight to the duke.

At night, the thief climbed to the duke's bedchamber and hissed at the window. The duke went to the window and the thief pushed him over the ledge. The duchess was scared and ran from the room.

The thief snatched the sheet and escaped. He gave it to the duke the next day. The duke pardoned him. The thief promised that he would be a good man from then on.

29. Johnny and the Maid

Once, there lived a small boy called Johnny.

One day, Johnny was playing with his ball in the kitchen. The maid was washing dishes. Suddenly, the ball hit a tray full of beautiful crockery and broke every piece. Johnny was scared and ran away.

Just then, Johnny's mother entered the kitchen. She saw the broken crockery and thought that the maid had broken them. She shouted, "This was my dear mother's dinner set! How could you break it into pieces! I cannot forgive you. Leave the house at once!"

The poor maid quietly went to her room to pack her bag.

Meanwhile, Johnny was standing behind the kitchen door. He heard everything. Then he saw the poor maid leaving the house. He ran to his mother and told her everything.

His mother stopped the maid at once. Since Johnny had told her the truth, she did not punish him, and the maid still had her job!

30. Ole-Luk-Oie - The Dream God

Ole-Luk-Oie knew so many stories. When good children were asleep, he would hold a bright umbrella over them. They would dream of beautiful stories.

While over the naughty children he would hold a plain umbrella and they wouldn't dream at all!

He came to a boy named Hjalmar for a week and told him a story every night. On Monday, he pointed out to Hjalmar, the awkwardness in his writing.

On Tuesday, he took him into a picture frame where he saw and felt many beautiful sights. On Wednesday night he took him sailing.

On Thursday, Ole-Luk-Oie took him dressed as a tin soldier to a mouse's wedding.

On Friday, they attended the dolls' wedding. On Saturday, he showed him chinamen.

Finally on Sunday, he told him of his brother, who told frightful stories to those who were bad. So Hjalmar decided to be good always.

31. The Golden Treasure

Once, there lived a drummer. One day, his wife went to the church to get her son christened. The little boy was named Peter. His mother called him her "Golden Treasure."

The drummer wanted his son to join the army and win a silver cross while his mother wanted him to sing with the choir at the church. Eventually, Peter joined the army and went to fight the war.

All this while, his mother worried about the safety of her "Golden Treasure." Many months later, Peter returned safely. Though he had not won the silver cross, both his parents were very happy.

Later, Peter went on to learn the violin and become a renowned musician. His father was no more but when he came home, Peter played his father's drums. His mother was proud of him, because he had fulfilled both his parents' wishes and was a good son.

1. Honest Hans

Once, a princess fell very ill. The doctors said that eating an apple would cure her. The king announced that whosoever cured her would marry her.

Hearing this, a farmer sent his two elder sons with apples. On the way, a man enquired what was in the basket. "Frog's legs," they said.

"So be it!" said the man. The elder sons walked away, but little did they know that the man was a magician, who was testing their honesty.

They reached the palace and found frog's legs inside the basket! They ran off before they were beaten.

Now the third son, Hans, decided to try his luck. On his way, Hans also met the man who enquired what was in the basket. Honest Hans said, "Apples."

"So be it!" said the man.

With a single bite of Hans' apple, the princess recovered! The overjoyed king married Hans to his daughter.

2. The Saucy Boy

Once, on a cold, rainy night, a poet was sitting by his fireplace. He thought, "I am glad I do not fall in love. It could break my heart and make my life sad!" Suddenly, he heard a knock on the door.

Standing outside, was a wet and cold boy. He had beautiful, curly hair, which made him look like an angel. The boy was holding a bow in his hand. Its colours had become wet in the rain and had run onto each other.

The poet allowed the boy inside his house and dried his wet hair. He also warmed his hands and gave him some warm milk to drink. Soon, a red glow spread over the boy's cheeks. He got up and started dancing around the poet.

The poet smiled at the merry boy and asked him, "What is your name?"

"My name is Cupid," answered the boy. "Don't you know me? I shoot with my bow."

The poet looked at the bow and said to the boy, "Your bow is spoilt, though."

Worried, the boy looked at the bow. However, his bow was not damaged and its string was pulled tight. To check, the boy pulled the string back and shot an arrow at the poet's heart.

As the poet fell on the floor in pain, he said aloud, "Ah! The Cupid has shot his arrow at me, and I have fallen in love! I will warn all boys and girls to keep away from the naughty Cupid, for he will make them fall in love too!"

Many years later, the poet told this story to his grandchildren, and said, "Children, that was when I found your grandmother. Then, many years later, Cupid came again and did the same with your mom and dad!"

3. The Spindle, the Shuttle and the Needle

Once, a girl lived with her godmother. The godmother taught her spinning, weaving and sewing. One day, the ailing godmother told her, "The house, spindle, shuttle and needle are yours. Always remember God and know that you are blessed. You will be fine." Then she died.

Thereafter, the girl worked hard and lived well and was happy.

A prince was looking for a bride who was poor yet very talented and intelligent.

One day, the girl saw him and promptly fell in love with him. She softly said, "Oh spindle, shuttle and needle, please make the prince marry me!"

The spindle jumped and ran away. The shuttle wove a beautiful carpet outside the house. The needle cleaned the house. The prince followed the dancing spindle to the girl's house. He fell in love with the simply dressed girl, surrounded by such beauty. He married her at once!

4. The Proud Princess

A proud princess lived in a huge castle. She could see her entire kingdom clearly from the huge castle windows. She said to her suitors, "I shall marry you, but you have to hide from me on the first day of marriage. If I find you on that day, you shall be beheaded."

Thus, the princess married many times and then beheaded all her husbands, as she always spotted them from the huge castle windows.

Finally, she married a handsome young man. The man went to hide in the forest. There, he pulled a thorn from a lame fox's foot. In return, the fox told him how he could turn into a fly and hide in the princess' hair.

The princess looked but could not find him. The next day, the man became himself and stood before her. He had fulfilled her condition. They remained married and lived happily for ever.

5. The Lucky Thief

Once, there lived a beautiful princess.

One day, while riding, the princess accidentally stepped on a witch's toes. The witch at once cursed her, "You shall marry a rabbit!"

Unknown to the princess, there was a handsome young thief who knew how to magically turn himself into a rabbit. He had successfully robbed many houses by doing so.

The thief decided to rob the castle. He became a rabbit and slipped into the castle at night.

He entered the princess' room and turned into a man and started opening drawers. Just then, the princess woke up. The thief quickly turned back into a rabbit. However, the princess thought that he would be her husband, hence caged him!

She ordered the priest to marry her to the rabbit. The shocked priest obeyed. As soon as the cage was opened, the rabbit turned into a handsome man! They were married and lived happily.

6. Strong Hank

Once, a boy called Hank and his mother lived in the thickest part of the forest. Ten years ago, they were captured by robbers, who had brought them there. They had been living as the robbers' slaves ever since.

Hank had grown up into a strong boy. One day, he asked his mother where their true home was. His mother said, "Our home is in a village. I wish we could escape and go there!"

Hank found a strong branch and hid it. At night, when the robbers were sleeping, Hank hit them on their heads. Then, he stuffed a sack with gold and jewels. Next, he and his mother ran away quickly.

They walked till they came to a pretty cottage in the village. A man stood outside and Hank's mother ran to him. The man recognised his wife and son, and hugged them. The family lived happily ever after.

7. Rick and the Goblin

Rick lived with his mother and father. He was a kind lad.

One day, an old goblin asked Rick for food. He gave him some, but the goblin was greedy, and Rick did not have more food.

The angry goblin snapped his fingers. Suddenly, Rick's hands and feet were tied and he stood inside a cave. Across him, was a beautiful princess, who was also tied.

The wicked goblin captured people who annoyed him and kept them as slaves.

Rick fell in love with the princess and decided to save her and everybody else. He struggled and soon broke open his ropes. When the goblin went out, Rick freed the princess and all the other people.

When the goblin returned, they all pounced on him and tied him with ropes.

Then, Rick took the princess to her father, the king. He was so happy that he married the princess to Rick.

8. The Old Man

Once, there was a woodcutter. One day, he came home empty-handed. He asked his elder daughter to go out and get food.

The elder daughter set out, but lost her way. She came to a house, where an old man lived with his goats. The elder daughter was hungry, so she cooked for herself, ate and slept.

The old man was angry at her selfishness and locked her in the cellar.

The next day, the younger daughter went to look for her sister. She reached the old man's house. There, she cooked food, then fed the old man and his goats. Then, she ate and slept.

The next morning, she woke up in a plush bed. There was a palace where the hut had been.

The old man was actually a handsome, young prince. The kind younger daughter had removed the curse that was on him, so he happily married her.

9. The Poor Boy

There was once a little boy who lost his parents. The magistrate declared that the miller would take care of him.

The miller brought him home. His mean wife was unhappy and complained, "One more mouth to feed!" Then the boy was told to mind the chickens.

A hawk flew away with the mother hen, and the boy was scolded and beaten and not given food. He tied all the chicks together. However, the hawk took those also.

Tired of being beaten, the boy ran away. In the churchyard, he found some food to eat. He crawled into an open grave and slept. The cold night air chilled him and he died. He turned into an angel and appeared before the miller and his wife. He said, "You shall never have your own child, for you are neither loving nor caring."

The couple had to suffer, for being mean to children.

103

10. The Corn Cobs

God gave man corn to grow as food. Each plant grew hundreds of cobs. Men had plenty of food and they grew careless.

God watched as men paid less and less attention to their food crops. The cornfields grew well and there was lots of corn. Men picked some cobs and left the rest.

One day, a mother and daughter were in the fields. The mother was picking corn. The daughter was playing and fell into a puddle, dirtying her clothes.

The mother, who had washed many clothes that morning, plucked a few cobs and cleaned her daughter's dress using them.

God was furious. "No more corn for you!" he thundered. The number of cobs on each plant decreased.

The men begged for God's mercy. God said, "I am giving you one final chance."

Since then, men have received small amounts of corn, but have always thanked God for their food.

11. The Prince and the Witch

There was a king who had a handsome son. The prince liked seeing new and strange buildings. Thus, once, he made a slippery glass bridge and visited it every day. He enjoyed using it as a slide.

However, one day, as the prince was climbing it, he slipped and fell into a crack. He kept sliding till a wicked witch caught him. She made him her servant. Thus, the prince lived deep under the ground.

The witch had a magical ladder that she used, to go above the ground. The prince longed to see sunlight, be comfortable, eat good food and meet his parents.

So, one day, when the witch slept, he stole her wand and magic hat. Now, she was powerless and he took the ladder. He climbed out and the king and queen rushed to hug him. He burnt the witch's wand and hat, but kept the magical ladder.

12. The True Bride

There was a lovely girl who loved a man truly. The man promised to marry her after a month.

"I will wait for you under the lime tree," she said to him and kissed him on his left cheek. "Do not let anyone kiss you on your left cheek."

When the man went home, he saw a beautiful woman who asked him to marry her. He refused, for he truly loved the girl.

So, the woman, who was actually a witch, cast a spell on him by saying, "You will forget your true love!" The man forgot the girl and wandered about.

After a month, the girl went to the lime tree. However, the poor man had forgotten everything and did not come. The girl searched for him. She found him in another town. She rushed and kissed his left cheek.

The man's memory returned. They got married and lived happily.

13. The Dryad

A fairy called Dryad lived on a tree. She had heard about the wonders of Paris and she fell in love with the city. She longed to go there.

One night, Dryad saw a spark fly out of the moon. The moon guard came to her and told her that her desire would cause her harm. She would go to Paris, and become a human. Thus, she would die soon. Dryad did not worry and still desired to go to Paris.

So one day, Dryad's tree was dug out and carried to the city of Paris to be planted in place of a dead tree. Dryad wanted to go to every corner of Paris. Thus, she was converted to a human lady for a day. However, as she travelled, she saw how Paris had changed for the worse with pollution and lesser trees. The next morning, Dryad died of sorrow.

14. The Parson and the Thief

A thief and the parson's daughter loved each other. The thief asked for the parson's permission to marry her.

The parson refused. His daughter said, "Father, I beg you! Let us marry. I will make him an honest man."

The parson then challenged the thief, "You can marry my daughter if you place my priest in a sack in the bell tower."

The thief went to the church that night. He stuck lit candles on the backs of crabs. Then opening a large sack, he shouted, "The Devil is here! Save yourself!" The priest came running out. He saw the lit candles moving about slowly, and was frightened. He ran towards the thief.

The thief stuffed him in the sack and dragged him to the top of the bell tower.

The next morning, the parson saw the priest emerge from the sack in the bell tower. He married his daughter to the thief.

15. The Fearless Man

There was a beautiful princess, who was imprisoned by a wicked dragon, on top of a very high mountain.

The dragon found her very pretty, so he had taken her to his home. He made her do all the housework, which she hated because she had never done any work in her life.

The king had offered a big reward to anyone who could rescue her.

A fearless man knew all about the dragon. He went to the mountain top, crossing many dangers. Then, he rescued the princess, when the dragon was away.

The king was happy and so was the princess. She begged the fearless man to marry her, but he said to the king, "Sir, she hates housework and I am not rich enough to keep servants."

The king gave him a huge mansion, many servants and lots of money. Thereafter, the fearless man and the princess lived happily.

16. The Happiest of All

Once, there was a rose bush with lovely roses. One day, the wind decided to see what life all those roses lived, to decide which one was the happiest.

One day, a mother, who had lost her daughter, came to the rose bush. She plucked a rose, placed it on her daughter's grave and kissed it.

Then, an old woman came and plucked another rose and took it home. She wanted to preserve it as a dry flower, so that it would stay forever.

Next, a man strolled into the garden and plucked a rose. He wrote a poem on the rose so that he would be remembered always.

The last rose on the bush said it was the happiest because it had stayed with its mother bush till the end.

Since, the other roses had been put to good use also, the wind decided that all of them were happy.

17. The Porter's Son

Once, there lived a General. He lived in a grand house with his wife and daughter, Emily. In the cellar of the same house, a porter lived with his family. The porter had a son named George.

As children, the General would allow George to dance and entertain Emily. As George grew, he practised his painting and went to Rome to study further. George excelled as a painter and he was praised everywhere. Still, he did not forget Emily and would send her all his paintings.

When George returned, he asked the General for Emily's hand in marriage. However, the General was furious and he refused. Then, one day Emily went to a fancy ball and met George there. They both danced together. When the General saw them, he invited George for dinner.

At dinner, he spoke to George and realised that he was a good man. Thus, he happily allowed Emily to marry George.

18. The Tea-Tray

Once, there was a boy called Charlie.

Now, Charlie really wanted a sledge. All his friends had one. Even little Toddy Graham boasted about it. Thus, Charlie went to his aunt and requested her to buy him and his sister, Molly, a sledge. However, aunt refused and asked him to play with his other toys instead.

This annoyed Charlie. Thus, he took one of aunt's new tea-trays to use as a sledge. Charlie and Molly's first ride downhill was a success; but on the second one, Charlie could not steer it properly, and – Wham! They crashed into Toddy Graham's sledge. Aunt's tray crashed into pieces. Poor Molly was hurt!

Charlie felt very guilty, and took care of his sister. He saved his pocket money and bought his aunt a new tray. Aunt gifted both of them a sledge on Christmas. They understood why she had refused to get it earlier!

19. Runaway Nest

Once, a family of birds lived in the forest. The parent birds would go looking for food for themselves and their babies every day.

One day, when the parent birds were away to look for food, a hailstorm occurred. The heavy rain and strong wind caused their nest to blow away and land on the branch of a tree far away.

When the mother bird returned, she could not find her nest. She tried to look for it in vain. She called out to the father bird and sobbed, "I cannot find our nest!"

He tried to comfort her and began searching.

They searched the place where their tree stood, but were unable to locate it. Thus, they decided to look further away and flew high. After searching for a long time, they found their nest on another tree. They saw that the babies were safe. Happily, they hugged them!

20. The Boy Who Became a Robin

According to Raghu's family tradition, every young lad had to go on a long fast to have a guardian angel. The time had come for Raghu, a young Indian boy, to meet his angel.

Raghu's father was very religious, and wanted his son to have the best guardian angel. Hence, he asked Raghu to fast for twelve days.

Fasting for twelve days was difficult for Raghu. On the last few days, he begged his father to let him eat, as he feared he would die of hunger. However, his father insisted that he carry on. On the twelfth day, the father went to his son with food, but by then, Raghu was already talking to his guardian angel, who had decided to punish the cruel father.

As a punishment to his father, the guardian angel turned Raghu into a robin forever, to sing sweet songs far away from his father.

21. The Truthful Dove

A long time ago, a dove and a bat set out on a journey across many forests. One night, a storm raged in a forest, and they were unable to find shelter.

Just then, an owl came to them and offered them his house as shelter, for he never slept at night. The bat and the dove readily agreed. However, the owl was selfish. Although he let them inside his house, he was very rude to them.

The cunning bat falsely praised the owl for a long time, for he thought that this way, the owl would be polite to him. On the other hand, the dove kept quiet and did not lie.

Suddenly, the owl turned into a beautiful white snowy owl and said, "I was testing both of you. The honest dove has won my test!" Thus, he rewarded the dove and left the cunning bat with nothing. Since then the bat had to stay awake in the night with the owl, while the dove slept peacefully!

22. The Eagle

One day, all the birds in the forest, the eagle, the sparrow, the lark, the robin, the cuckoo, the lapwing and many others decided that they should appoint a king.

After much discussion, they decided that the one who was the strongest should be made the king. The eagle flew the highest, and was made the king.

However, the eagle was very dull witted and lazy. Under his rule, the Bird Kingdom suffered. Thieves flew around freely, and nothing was done to catch them. The hailstorm destroyed the birds' nests, but nothing was done to help them. Thus, all birds were unhappy and homeless.

Then, they realised their mistake. They said, "The eagle is the strongest, but it does not mean that the he is a good king. We want a new king!" Thus, the wise owl was made the king, and the birds lived happily under his fair rule.

23. The Old Woman Who became a Woodpecker

Far away in Northland, an old saint was walking through a village to go to the mountains. After a while, he grew tired of walking. He also felt hungry. Thus, he knocked on a lonely cottage.

The cottage belonged to an old woman who was baking cakes right then. The saint requested the woman for some cake to eat. However, she was miserly and heartless. She gave him three very tiny cakes.

Just as the saint was leaving, she thought she had given him too much! Thus, she took them all back.

The saint was very angry, as he was weak and tired, and cursed the woman, "You are cruel, and pitiless! You shall only survive on berries and nuts, and bore through wood all your life." Just as he said this, the woman turned into a woodpecker. You can see one boring tirelessly through the wood for food!

24. Grandfather's Picture Book

Grandfather knew a lot of stories. He was from Copenhagen. He had made several picture books, in which he pasted pictures from books and newspapers, or those drawn by hand.

Once, grandfather showed the children his most precious picture book. On its first page was written, 'The memorable year when gas replaced the old oil lamps in Copenhagen.'

Grandfather explained that the people of Copenhagen had earlier used oil lamps and then decided to start using the gas lamps. In his dream, he had heard an old oil lamp talking to other oil lamps that all the old lamps had seen many years. They were very knowledgeable and that they liked to tell the stories of their ancestors to others.

This gave grandfather the idea of making picture books, which contained all the events in the history of Copenhagen. Thus, he was able to tell many stories to others, like the lamps.

25. The Scratch Team

Once, there was a boy called Tom. He lived with his parents. Poor Tom was very shy and so he did not have any friends.

Then, one day, Aunt Gertrude came to meet him. He loved his aunt greatly, so he told her how he wanted to play with the boys in the neighbourhood, but was scared to join them.

The next day, Aunt Gertrude went with Tom to the neighbourhood. There she started calling out to children to come and play ball with them. Soon, a lot of boys came forward and started playing.

Now, every day, the boys would get together in the afternoons and play till tea-time. Aunt Gertrude called them 'The Scratch Team.'

Tom was very happy. He had friends now. Most of them even went to the same school as him. Tom thanked Aunt Gertrude, for she had helped him make good friends!

26. Was it a Dream?

Once, a boy called Ron lived with his brother Frank and their parents.

One day, Frank decided to go fishing. When the boys reached the pool, Frank started fishing. Ron sat waiting for Frank, for he did not like fishing.

So he lay down next to the stream. He moved closer to the water and noticed many fish grouped together, talking about something. One very small fish wanted to taste the worm on Frank's bait, but his mother forbade him. Ron wanted to tell the little fish that his mother was right!

He woke up with a start, and saw an excited Frank winding his chord. He realised that the little fish was caught by the bait.

Just then, Frank slipped, and fell on the ground and lost the little fish in the water. Ron felt sorry for Frank, but was glad that the little fish was now safe!

27. The Tailor Who Lied

Once, an ordinary tailor killed seven flies and sewed a victory message on his shirt that read, 'Seven At Once.' People thought that he had killed seven people at once!

The king heard about him and tested him. The tailor told the king that he had a rock in his fist, but it was actually a lump of cheese. Then, he squeezed it into pulp.

Next, the tailor held a bird in his fist, and said that it was a rock. He threw it hard, saying it would not return. The bird flew away, and did not return.

The king was so impressed with him that he married the tailor to the princess.

They lived happily. But once, in his sleep, the tailor murmured, "A patch here, a patch there!"

The princess realised that he was just a tailor! The king's men beat him and he decided never to lie again.

28. Philip Charmed

Philip was a young man. He was a cheerful, handsome and a kind man. Everybody had a good word to say about Philip.

Once, Philip had to attend a party in the evening. The people were looking forward to a delicious dinner and merry dancing.

At the party, Philip was standing in the corner and tapping his foot to the music. Suddenly, he spotted the prettiest girl in the room. He watched her dancing gaily.

Philip was charmed by the beautiful girl. He walked up to her and asked her for a dance. They danced together the entire evening. All eyes in the room followed the couple.

Philip had never enjoyed dancing so much with anyone. He wanted to dance for a long time with the charming girl.

Philip then asked the girl to marry him. The girl smiled and said, "Yes." Thereafter, Philip and the girl were happily married.

29. Peiter, Peter and Peer

The Pietersens were an extremely nice family. Their father was one of the thirty-two members of the town council and this was considered to be an honour. He had three sons – Peiter, Peter and Peer. The three boys set ambitions for themselves.

Peiter wanted to become a robber. He was convinced that the life of a robber was the most interesting. Peter wanted to become a trash collector. Peer simply wanted to become "Papa."

Sadly, Peiter became quarrelsome as he grew, like a robber. Once, he even intentionally dropped tea on his mother's new silk dress.

However, as the boys grew older, they became wise, and gave up their childhood dreams. All three got respectable jobs.

Peer became inclined towards science. He would collect frogs and snakes and perform experiments. His elder brothers got married but Peer decided not to marry and he never did, till he died.

30. The Little Green Ones

Once, there was an apple tree that used to be green and blooming. Of late, creatures dressed in green uniforms were eating it up.

A man spoke to one of the creatures. The creature told him that he belonged to a family of very strange creatures, who liked to be called, "The Little Green Ones." In fact, their family did not like humans at all because the humans called them by rude names. They did not like this. Also, it complained that humans killed them with soap water.

These Little Green Ones were born on trees and spent their whole life on them. They blamed the humans for eating all the different types of green plants, which grew around the tree.

The man, who had come to wash the tree with soap water did not do so and went back. He then remembered that humans called these creatures "Tree Lice."

1. Phil and the Snake

Once, there lived a young man called Phil. He loved everyone and was never unkind to anyone.

One day, Phil heard noises outside his window. He went out and saw a large crowd. The crowd was gathered to watch a huge white snake.

The crowd was scared. "We must get rid of this snake!" they said.

However, Phil said, "Kind people, please do not kill the poor thing. Here, I will take it." Then, he scooped the white snake in a large bowl and took it inside his house. There, he took great care of the snake. Surprisingly, the snake did not hiss or bite Phil.

The next morning, Phil woke up and saw a beautiful princess standing before him. She said, "Kind Phil, a wicked witch had cursed me and I thus became a white snake. Your kindness broke the curse!"

Thereafter, Phil and the princess were married.

2. The Water Spirit Boy

Once, a farmer was working on his farm. Suddenly, the wicked Water Spirit of the well appeared before him. She said, "I will give you plenty of riches, if you will give me what was born in your house today."

The farmer agreed blindly. However, when he returned home, he was shocked to hear that his wife had had a baby boy!

The farmer kept quiet about his promise to the Water Spirit. He was frightened and moved to another town. The boy was kept away from wells, and the farmer grew richer and richer! Soon, the boy turned into a fine young man. He was engaged by the count to be his official hunter.

One day, while hunting a deer, the man went near the Water Spirit's well. He stretched out his hand for water, and the Water Spirit recognised him and pulled him in.

The man's mother was upset that her husband had promised the Water Spirit their son. She asked a wise old woman what she could do to save her son. The woman gave her a golden spinning wheel and a thistle. She told her to spin on a full moon night and sleep by the well. If the Water Spirit appeared, she was to throw the thistle at her feet.

The woman did what she was told and when she had spun lots of thread, she went to sleep. After a while, her son emerged from the well. He pulled himself up by the thread. Screaming with anger, the Water Spirit followed.

The mother quickly threw the thistle at the Water Spirit's feet. It sprang into a huge, prickly bush and the Water Spirit howled in pain. She could not move as she was stuck! The mother and her son ran far away to safety.

3. The Little Boy

Once, a little boy lived in an orphanage. One winter evening, he sat in his cold room and shivered. To distract himself, he thought of all the nice things.

He first saw himself sitting on a large sofa by a large iron stove. He saw his dead parents sitting with him. The little boy stretched out his feet to warm them.

He then imagined himself in a dining room. The table was covered with a snowy white table-cloth. There was a steaming roast goose, stuffed with apple and a large plum cake with chocolate icing on the table. Suddenly, the goose jumped down from the dish and waddled across the floor, with a knife and fork stuck to it, towards the little boy.

Then the boy imagined himself under a Christmas tree that had numerous wrapped gifts. Each one was for him. Happy with his thoughts, the little boy was fast asleep.

4. The Special Bean

Once, there lived a boy. He always asked his uncle when he would grow up. His uncle would say, "When you are wise, you will become a man. Take this bean. It will help you at the right time, but use it wisely."

Time passed by and the boy decided to leave home to earn his fortune. The day he was leaving, his uncle fell ill. The boy decided not to leave, but wondered how to help his uncle.

Then, he remembered the bean and planted it. At once, a huge climber laden with beans sprang up. The boy picked a bean and said, "I wish this was money. Then I could buy medicines with it to cure my uncle." It turned into money! It was a magic wish-granting bean!

The boy bought the medicines and ran to his uncle. His uncle said, "You did wisely, son. Now you are really a man!"

5. The Woman and the Wizard

Once upon a time, a wizard stole a woman's baby. The woman ran after the wizard but lost him. She asked an old woman, "Have you seen a wizard with my baby?"

The old woman replied, "Yes, but I will tell you only if you sing a song for me." So the woman sang and the old woman told her the way.

She went further and asked a thorn-bush about the wizard. The thorn-bush said, "I will not tell you until you have warmed me in your bosom. I am freezing to death here." The woman pressed the thorn-bush to her bosom to warm it till the thorns pierced her flesh and drops of blood flowed. The thorn-bush parted and she could see where the wizard was hiding.

Finally, the woman reached the wizard. He said, "I saw your efforts to find your baby. I will never trouble a mother or her child now!" and he gave her baby back.

6. Wonderful George

Once, there lived a boy called George.

One night, George's father had gone out for some work. George's mother had very high fever. Thus, he at once left home and ran to bring the doctor. Suddenly, it started raining heavily. The night was very dark and George was wet and cold. While running down the hill, he fell and hurt his head on a stone.

Poor George was so hurt that he fainted. While returning home, his father found George lying on the ground and took him to the doctor. When George woke up, he asked the doctor to go and check on his mother.

Thus, George, with a bandage on his head, his father and the doctor went in a carriage to his home. There, the doctor gave his mother some medicine and she was better soon.

George's parents were very happy to have such a wonderful son!

7. The Sparrow and the Blackberry Bush

Once, there was a beautiful blackberry bush near a pond. Near it lived a small family of sparrows. The berries told each other how lucky they were to have the sparrows as their neighbours.

However, the sparrow family did not like the blackberry bush and thought that they were very foolish. The sparrows would all make fun of their neighbours secretly. One day, the mother sparrow went to find food but some naughty boys caught her in a net. They wanted to catch a parrot but caught her as she looked pretty.

They kept the mother sparrow without food or water for many days. Finally, they got bored and set her free. However, she was so weak that she could barely fly. She tried her best to reach her home, but fell down before reaching it. Fortunately, she fell into the blackberry bush. Her neighbours acted like a cushion for her till her family came to her rescue.

8. The Portrait

Once, a boy named John lived with his parents. Across the street, lived an old man in an old house.

One day, John decided to meet the old man, so he rang the bell. The old man invited John in.

John saw a picture of a beautiful lady on the wall in the living room. The lady in the picture looked young and gay. John said, "Who is this in the picture?"

The old man replied, "Oh! She was the most beautiful woman in our town! I loved her many years ago. She has been dead nearly half a century."

John and the old man talked for a long time. After a few months, John sadly saw people carry him away in a coffin. The old house and all its objects were sold. John bought the lady's portrait and hung it in his room, in memory of his old friend.

9. The Sailor Doll

There was a doll that wore trousers and a sailor's cap. He had broken his neck, in an attempt to jump off the table, and was put away in the drawer.

He was a proud doll, who thought he was no less than a human, as he had arms and legs, eyes and mouth. He remembered how children would put him in his boat and he would sail in the bathtub, and sighed.

Then, one day, someone opened the drawer and picked him up. "This doll will be fine. I will stitch his neck." A needle poked his neck and stitched him up. He felt as good as new!

Then, a boy's small hand clutched him tightly and he looked up. "You are a sailor," said the boy to him, "so you shall sail."

The boy placed him in a boat and patted him encouragingly. Both played happily for hours.

10. Peter's Animal Kingdom

Once, there lived a boy called Peter. From a very young age, Peter was interested in Science. He had a small cabinet where he kept many small animals as pets, like rats, butterflies and even earthworms.

Then one day, he observed a spider living on his windowsill. He observed that a spider would weave his web to catch flies. Then, to his horror, he noticed that the female spider ate her husband after laying eggs.

When Peter saw this, he grew very thoughtful. How could a creature eat another creature of its own kind? He found this very odd. However, when he read his books, Peter realised that it was very normal for all spiders to behave like this. He learned that sometimes, the male spiders themselves helped the female spiders to eat them!

Thus, Peter understood that different creatures behaved differently. He felt very amazed at Mother Nature's ways.

11. The Old Lamp

Once, there was an old lamp in the church.

On his last night of service, three candidates who wished to take his position approached the old lamp.

The first was a herring's head, which could emit light in the darkness. Next was a piece of rotten wood, which shone in the dark. The third was a glow-worm. It could give bright light.

The old lamp said that none of them could take his place. Before he could say more, all three called him names and left.

The next day, a modern oil lamp replaced the lamp. When the three candidates saw the old lamp being carried away, they realised their mistake.

They went to the old lamp and said, "Brother, the humans decided who would replace you. We should not have spoken without knowing the whole truth. We are very sorry."

The old lamp forgave them.

12. The Gardener and the Manor

Once, a rich family owned a beautiful manor in the country. They spent their summer holidays in this manor.

The manor was beautifully carved and had lovely rare flowers in its garden. The flowers blossomed under the care of the hard-working gardener. He loved the garden and his hard work bore results when large fruits and colourful flowers grew.

Everyone in the neighbourhood praised the gardener. The apples, pears and melons he grew were of excellent quality and were sold for a very high price in the markets. His knowledge about herbs, flowers and fruits was great. Often, people came to ask him about a particular plant or herb.

The master of the manor admired the gardener's knowledge about flowers. He was very proud of his gardener. The gardener was a faithful servant and continued working hard without complaints.

13. The Old Man and His Wife

Once, an old man lived with his wife in a small hut. They were poor but loved each other a lot. One day, the wife sent him to sell their cow in the market for some money. The man went with his friend.

There, he sold the cow in exchange for a colourful parrot. His friend warned, "Your wife needed money. She will be very angry with you."

The man replied, "She always agrees with what I do. I bet she will like the parrot."

The friend was not convinced and promised him hundred gold coins if his wife did not scold him.

After they reached home, the wife saw the parrot and said, "My husband always takes the right decision. I am sure whatever he did is good for us."

The friend was amazed and gave the man hundred gold coins. The man and his wife were very happy.

14. Months in the Year

Once, an old man sat in a chair in his room. His grandson came to him and asked, "How many months are there in a year?"

The old man said, "There are twelve months in a year."

The grandson was amazed and said, "How are seasons divided in these months?"

The old man said, "Every month has its specialty. Winter season starts with November. Everything around is cold and frozen. The spring starts in February and flowers blossom everywhere. With April begins summer. It is hot and dusty then. In August, autumn season starts. It ends in October and then winter is here again. So, this is how the seasons are divided in the twelve months of the year."

The grandson said, "Wow! God has created such beautiful seasons to fill our life with variety."

The old man smiled and said, "God is great in every way."

15. The Beetle and the Horse

Once, a horse lived in the emperor's stable. He was extremely beautiful and had fought great battles. So, the emperor gave him gold shoes.

A beetle also lived in the stable. He and the horse were good friends. One day, the beetle noticed the horse's shoes. He said, "Dear horse, I also want gold shoes."

The horse replied, "You have very thin legs. So, such shoes would be very heavy and uncomfortable for you."

The beetle was angry with the horse. The horse could not see his friend upset and requested the emperor for gold shoes for him.

The beetle wore the shoes and was very happy. However, he could not fly because they were too heavy. He cried, "Please help me horse. I cannot fly in these shoes!"

The horse felt sorry and requested the emperor's men to remove the shoes. The beetle realised that he should not be greedy!

16. The Old Man's Neighbour

Once, a child was walking down the street when saw an old man faint just outside his house. He took him inside and called a doctor. The doctor told him that the old man would not live for long.

The child felt bad for him and left for home. However, he visited him every day. Despite the care, the old man died a few days later.

One day, the child's father lost his job. Now, the family did not have money and starved. Thus, the child was about to faint with hunger. Suddenly, he saw the old man dressed in white clothes, like an angel. He placed his cool hand on the child's forehead and disappeared.

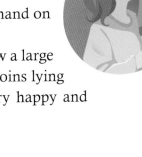

As the old man vanished, the child saw a large sack of food and a small pouch of gold coins lying beside him. The child's parents were very happy and proud of their child's kindness.

17. The Clay Pig

The clay pig was fat and full of coins. He sat importantly on the top of the cupboard. One day, the toys decided to hold a play, like the humans do. Everyone was asked over for a tea party and a play, and the pig was also given a written invitation.

The audience gathered. The toy soldiers sat in the front row and the paintings and the walking stick in the back row. The pig watched from the top of his cupboard.

The play got over and everyone clapped. The pig got very excited and thought he would reward the best actor. He tried to jump and push a few coins out, but instead, he tipped over and smashed to bits.

As they collected the coins, the toys said, "Ah, what a sad end!" All that was left of the excited fat clay pig was the broken pieces in the dustbin.

18. The Kind Angel

Once, a sailor was far from home. He missed his home and his mother and wife. It was winter and it snowed heavily.

The sailor lay in his bed, worrying about his family's health in the bitter winter. Suddenly, he saw a bright flash of silver light and an angel appeared in front of him. She smiled at him and he saw his dearest wife and his mother, busy at work. They looked happy and healthy. This vision faded. The sailor smiled and went to sleep.

In his country home, his mother and wife also saw a silver light through the kitchen window. There stood an angel and behind her, was a picture. It was the sailor, lying in bed, sleeping and smiling, as if dreaming. A letter was kept near his pillow.

The next day, the wife received her husband's letter. Though living separately, the angel brought the family close!

19. The Student

Once, a very intelligent student lived in a city. He heard that a great and wise teacher lived in a town nearby. He decided to go and see him.

Arriving at the teacher's house, he said, "Sir, you are the wisest teacher that I have heard of. Please teach me."

The teacher asked him about his home, his parents, his studies and what he liked to do. He then asked someone to bring tea for them.

The student offered to pour the tea. The teacher smiled and said, "I will do it." Then, he kept pouring the tea until his cup overflowed. The student said, "Sir, the cup is overflowing."

The teacher said, "Yes, like this cup, you are full of knowledge. You must practise it. Otherwise, it will be wasted, like this tea."

The student understood that the teacher was right and thanked him. Thus, he started teaching little children in a school.

20. The Best Pearl

A baby boy was born in a cottage. His mother wept joyfully.

The angel of the house counted the pearls that God had kept aside for the child. There was happiness, beauty, joy… Hey, wait!

"One pearl is missing. I know where it is," said the baby boy's angel. "We must fetch it!" said the angel of the house, and they went to find the missing pearl.

They flew to a house where a beautiful lady lay in a coffin. Her family was weeping. An angel in white was sitting there. A tear rolled down her cheeks and became a pearl. The baby's angel seized it and she and the angel of the house flew back to the house.

The angel of the house said, "This is a sorrow pearl. How can it be good?" The baby's angel replied, "Unless he knows sorrow, he will not value the happiness!"

21. The Washerwoman

There was a poor washerwoman who had once loved the mayor's younger brother. The mayor's mother had ordered her to marry someone else, because she was too poor for them. So, the sad washerwoman married a glove maker. He was a good man and they lived together happily. Soon, they had a boy.

Meanwhile, the mayor's younger brother went abroad. Soon after, the glove maker died, and the washerwoman had to work very hard to earn money. She wanted her boy to live a happy life. The little boy would also help her, but she grew weak.

One day, her friend told her that mayor's younger brother had passed away. The poor washerwoman was shocked and died soon after.

The younger brother had left a lot of money for the washerwoman. Her wishes for her boy came true. Thus, her boy lived very comfortably.

22. The Green Peas

There were five peas in a pod. Since they were green and everything around them was green, they thought the whole world was green!

The pea pod burst and out flew the peas in all directions. One rolled away and was quickly gobbled up by a hungry bird.

Two peas wanted to travel and see the world, but they fell into a flowerbed and were buried beneath the soil. Later, they sprouted into two lovely pea plants.

The fourth pea fell into the washing sink and lay in the water and swelled and swelled. It thought, "I cannot get any fatter. I am the fattest pea I know. I shall burst with joy!" The lady who was washing dishes poked the pea and it burst.

The last pea landed on a girl's hand. She said, "I will plant it in my flower pot." And so the last pea smiled contentedly and slept.

23. A Heart of Gold

Once, there lived a boy called Hans. He could not walk as he did not have feet.

Hans had a beautiful black nightingale, which sang him melodious songs. One day, while he was sitting in his room reading a book, a wicked cat entered the room and sat staring at the bird. Hans knew that the cat wanted to eat his nightingale and screamed at it, but the cat would not move. So, Hans threw the book at the cat, but she escaped and jumped to reach the cage. The cage fell down and the nightingale inside fluttered helplessly.

Hans did not think about himself and jumped out of his chair. Though he fell hard, he picked up the cage.

The nightingale was actually Hans' angel. Seeing Hans' selflessness, it gave him a pair of golden feet to reward his golden heart. Kind Hans could walk and run now!

24. Too Sweet

There was a boy called Jack. He was very fond of sweets. When all the other elders refused to give him chocolates and sweets, he would sneak into the kitchen and steal chocolates and candies from the jars. He did not brush his teeth properly, either.

Jack's parents would tell him not to eat too many sweets as they were harmful for health, but he never listened to them.

One day, Jack ate all the sweets from the jar while his parents were away. In the evening, he felt a terrible stomachache. His parents called the doctor. He said, "This is because you ate too many sweets, Jack!"

The next day, Jack felt a terrible toothache. His parents took him to the dentist. The dentist said, "You ate too many sweets, Jack!"

Now Jack learnt his lesson. Then on, he ate sweets only sometimes, and brushed his teeth properly.

25. Croak

Once, some fish lived in a pond.

One day, the fish decided to start a newspaper for themselves, like the one humans read. It would provide them with information about the Pond Kingdom.

The writers for the newspaper had been selected. However, there was great confusion while deciding the writer for the 'Jokes' section.

All the fish wanted someone funny to be the writer of the 'Jokes' section.

Then, the goldfish had an idea. He said, "Let us make the frog the writer! He looks funny and has a funny voice! He is the funniest creature, since he lives on both land and water. He is a half fish!"

All the fish started laughing at the goldfish's idea.

Another fish said, "The very thought of the frog makes us laugh! He should indeed be the joke writer!"

Thus, the frog was made the joke writer and the newspaper was named 'Croak'.

26. The Book

Once upon a time, there lived a wealthy family in a country mansion. On Christmas Eve, the family distributed presents and food to all their servants. The gardener, his wife and five children also got the presents. Everyone got clothes to wear, but the gardener's eldest son, Peter, received a book.

Peter was handicapped and he could not walk. The gardener was very unhappy as he thought that even Peter should have got clothes. He thought that the book was useless for him. However, Peter was very happy to receive a book as a present.

Now, Peter read wonderful stories from the book and narrated them to his parents. The gardener looked at his son's happy face while reading and thought, 'I was unhappy because I thought that the book was useless, but it makes my Peter so happy. May the rich family in the mansion be blessed!'

27. The Dream Palace

One night, the king dreamt of a palace that floated in the air. The king woke up and told his ministers about his dream. He said, "I will give twenty thousand gold coins to anyone who can build the floating palace for me."

The ministers made the announcement, since they were afraid of the king. The people, after hearing about the dream, said, "The king is foolish!"

The next day, an old man visited the king. "I've been robbed! I dreamed that I had a lot of money and one day, someone stole it. I've been ruined!"

The king laughed, "Ruined? You only dreamed of the money! You never really had it."

"Why, if your floating palace is a reality, then my money has been stolen. You are the king, catch those thieves!"

The king realised his own stupidity, and gave the old man ten gold coins.

28. The Three Travellers

Once, three young men, who were sons of farmers, wanted to make a lot of money quickly. So, they decided to trade with other lands and become rich.

They took all their money and travelled from place to place. They were able to make some money, but spent more money than they earned. After three years, they realised they had very little money left.

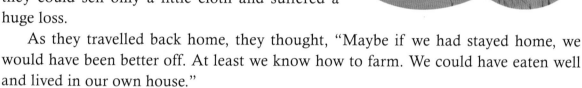

As a last try, they bought a lot of fine, woven cloth and started going from town to town, trying to sell it. Many other traders were also selling good cloth at the same time. Thus, they could sell only a little cloth and suffered a huge loss.

As they travelled back home, they thought, "Maybe if we had stayed home, we would have been better off. At least we know how to farm. We could have eaten well and lived in our own house."

29. The Trader's Sons

There was a rich trader. He had two sons. The younger son was his favourite, while he always scolded the elder son. When the sons grew up, the trader made the elder son work at the town square while the younger son was given good education.

The elder son made a lot of money at the town square. The trader thought, "He is doing so well without education. My younger son should do even better as he is educated!"

The trader asked the younger son to work at the town square too. However, he was lazy and never worked. Slowly, all his money was spent.

The trader said to his elder son, "Son, please help your brother."

The older son said, "Father, you loved him more. You help him. I have to look after myself." The trader realised his mistake but could do nothing.

30. The Snowman

A dashing snowman with a red scarf stood in the yard. His mouth was a rake with its teeth intact. He faced the house and children played around him. A robin sat down on his head.

The snowman looked curiously at the scene through the windows. In one corner, he saw beautiful red dancing shapes.

"What is that?" he asked the robin. "Fire! Look away, it will melt you," the robin chirruped.

Though the snowman did not understand why, but he wanted so much to touch the fire. He could not move, so, he looked longingly at the fire. As the sun shone, he melted slowly and was gone by the evening. All that was left was the shovel pole around which the snowman had been built. "It was the coal shovel pole! No wonder the poor snowman longed for the fire!" thought the robin.

31. The Slingshot

A brother and sister were playing in the garden. The brother was annoyed with his sister because she played with his toys.

"Give my slingshot back to me!" he said loudly and cuffed her on her ear. She cried and dropped it.

A little later, the brother had climbed the tree to check a bird's nest. Suddenly, the mother bird appeared and shrieked loudly. The brother tried to get down, but his trouser pocket got caught in a broken branch and he was stuck! The annoyed mother-bird pecked him all over.

"Do something!" he shouted at his sister. She slowly picked up the slingshot and aimed at the bird.

The mother-bird moved away and the brother freed his trouser pocket and descended quickly. He said to his sister, "I am so ashamed! I hit you, even then you saved me. Why?"

The sister simply said, "You are my brother and I love you!"

1. To Catch a Sunbeam

Jack was a young man who dreamed of becoming a writer. Jack's mother always encouraged him to write. She believed that ideas had to be caught, like catching a sunbeam.

One day, Jack sat at his writing table. Just then a bee came buzzing near his ear. He waved his hand to chase it away. The bee flew out of the window. Jack followed it out into the garden.

The bee flew to a gigantic beehive. When Jack looked into the entrance of the hive, he saw hundreds of bees in the passageways. They were busy flying up and down the passages. Some bees were making honey. Some bees were flying with baskets to collect pollen from flowers. The queen bee lay surrounded by her helpers.

Jack thought to himself, 'What a busy life the bees lead!'

Having caught the sunbeam, Jack sat down to write a tale about the bees.

2. Tears of Pearls

Once, there was a king who had three daughters.

One day, the king asked his daughters, "How much do you love me?" The elder daughters said that they loved him the most in the world. However, his youngest daughter answered, "Without salt, food is tasteless. I love my father like salt." The king was furious and banished her.

The youngest daughter wept tears of pearls as she left and was never heard of again.

Many years later, the king sent one of his counts to the forest for hunting. There, he met an old woman, carrying a heavy load. The kind count carried the woman's heavy load to her house. There, he met her ugly daughter. The daughter looked at him and went out to mind the geese.

The old woman gave him a little box with a single pearl inside, as a gift.

The count later went to the royal court. He remembered the gift and gave it to the queen. She opened the box and fainted. When she recovered, she told him that the pearl was exactly like what her daughter had wept, so many years ago.

The count promised he would look for the old woman. When he reached the old woman's house, he climbed a tree to watch. After a while, he heard sounds. He looked around and saw the ugly daughter take off her ugly skin. Lo and behold, she transformed into a beautiful girl with golden hair! The count was so surprised that he fell off the branch, and landed near the daughter's feet!

He got on his horse and rode to the palace, without stopping.

He brought the king and queen back. The king and queen embraced their daughter and thanked the old woman for looking after her. The count was rewarded handsomely, by the king, for reuniting them.

3. The Thistle's Wish

In a beautiful garden, there grew a single thistle among many trees. The lady of the house took flowers from the garden and kept them in a vase.

Despite its thorns, the thistle was covered in blossoms. The thistle looked lovely. Yet nobody touched the blossoms from fear of the thorns.

The thistle only had one wish. It wanted to be kept in the vase along with blossoms from the garden. Unfortunately, the thistle was overlooked time and again.

The thistle told every blossom on its tree about this wish.

The summer went by, and then autumn came. The leaves fell from the trees, and only a few flowers were left. A single flower bloomed near the roots of the thistle.

The lady of the house picked the flower, since there were no other pretty flowers and placed it in the vase. The thistle's wish was finally granted.

4. Uncle Harry

Richard's Uncle Harry was invited to judge a singing competition. Uncle wore his red cloak and fur boots and went to the auditorium.

Uncle was seated in the balcony of the auditorium. Suddenly, there was a cry of "Fire!" Smoke was coming from a side.

There was panic and as people rushed, Uncle Harry was trapped in the balcony. He called out but no one heard him. So he thought of jumping down. Uncle put one leg over the partition and one over the bench. Then, he sat there, as if on a horseback, in a bright red cloak, with one leg in a fur boot hanging out.

That was a sight to behold and in fact, someone did observe it and immediately sent help to the balcony. Thus, Uncle Harry did not have to jump down and was saved from burning. That was the most memorable evening of his life!

5. Freddy

Freddy was a talented painter. He loved the art gallery. He would think that there must be an art gallery in Heaven too. He felt that the many distinguished painters who had passed away, must have surely been painting the beautiful scenes in Heaven!

There was an art gallery close to Freddy's house. So deep was his love for art that even when he was very ill, he did not miss a single exhibition held there!

One day, Freddy fell very ill. The doctor prescribed that he put his feet in a bran bath one whole day. But Freddy had already decided to see an exhibition. Yet he followed the doctor's advice as well. He drove to the art gallery and sat with his feet in the bran bath there. People around him look surprised and stared at him, but Freddy sat there joyfully. He simply looked at the paintings as happily as ever!

6. Ice Maiden

Once, a little boy lived in the mountains with his cruel uncle. The uncle made him do all the household work and did not give him much to eat.

One day, the boy ran away from the house. There was snow all around. He reached the forest and sat under a tree. He was extremely tired and hungry. He closed his hands and prayed to God for help. Suddenly, he saw a young woman.

He asked, "Who are you?" She replied, "I am the Ice Maiden. Come with me." The boy followed her into a mountain cave. She gave him warm clothes to wear and delicious food to eat.

Then, she asked him, "Why were you sitting alone in the forest?" The boy told her of his cruel uncle. The Ice Maiden said, "You can stay with me from now on."

The boy thanked God for sending her to help him.

AUGUST

7. The Artist

Once, an artist lived in the ancient city of Rome. He made very beautiful paintings. However, he was not confident about his work and felt that people would not appreciate it. So, he never tried to sell his paintings and lived in poverty.

One day, a woman came to his place to get her portrait made. She was extremely beautiful. The artist was struck by her beauty and agreed. He painted her portrait in a week. When the woman saw it, she was very happy. She gave the artist good money and encouraged him to sell his paintings.

The artist finally agreed and sold them. People gave large sums of money in return and he became rich and popular.

After sometime, he went to the woman and thanked her. She said, "You were brilliant at your work but lacked confidence. Now you have it."

Later, they both got married and lived happily.

8. The Snail and the Rose Bush

Once, a snail lived under a rose bush. When people came near the bush to pluck flowers, the snail had to run around to save himself.

Slowly, he grew jealous and hated the bush, because people always praised the roses. One day, he said, "You think highly of yourself because people praise you. They step on me to pluck your flowers. I hate you!"

The bush replied, "People love me because I spread fragrance everywhere. Those who do good things, or do something for others are always appreciated."

The snail did not understand all this and wished the bush would die soon. After sometime, he requested a cow to destroy the bush. While destroying the bush, the thorns from the bush pricked the cow and she ran away. However, she accidentally stepped on the snail and killed it.

The bush felt sad for the snail but thought, "God punishes the ones who wish ill for others."

9. The Jealous Ducks and the Singing Bird

Once, a farmer had a duck farm. He sold the ducks' eggs in the market.

One day, the farmer went to sell the eggs and bought a little singing bird from the market. The bird had a very sweet voice. He gave her to the ducks for their amusement.

Every day, the ducks made the little bird sing for hours. The farmer loved his songs and brought expensive grains for her. So, some ducks grew jealous of her.

One day, they decided to kill the bird. They made her sing all day without food and water. By the evening, the little bird got exhausted and fell on the ground.

The ducks did not pity her and left the place. After some time, the farmer came and found the bird very ill!

He was very sad and thought, 'I should not have given this poor bird to these jealous ducks. I am sure they made him ill.'

10. The Winter Season

Once, a little boy and girl lived with their parents on the mountains. The boy and the girl played in the snow during winters.

One day, their father made a snowman for them. The snowman had a big and fat stomach and a small round face.

His eyes and nose were made with pieces of wood. Their father gave his old hat to be put on his head. Now, the children played around the snowman every day. It always smiled at them.

After some time, the season changed to summer. The sun shone bright in the sky and the snowman melted. The children were very sad.

Their father said, "Nature keeps changing. We should learn to enjoy all its beautiful seasons. Winter will come again and we will make another snowman."

The children understood and then on enjoyed all other seasons as much as winter.

11. The Old Man is Always Right

One day, an old man decided to sell his horse. His wife agreed and he set off.

On the way, the old man met someone who had two apples and exchanged the horse for it.

On his way back, he met two gentlemen who were carrying two sacks. The old man stopped to talk to them. They were curious about the apples that he was holding in his hands.

Hearing the entire story, the gentlemen said, "If your wife doesn't scold you for bringing two apples for a horse, we will give you a sack full of money." The old man agreed.

Then they all went to the old man's home. There, the wife saw the two apples in the man's hands. She happily said, "Just what our neighbours wanted! They are foreigners and do not get apples in their home country! We shall sell these to them now! You are always right!"

The gentlemen gave them money as promised. The old couple also sold the two apples to their foreigner neighbours and lived comfortably from then on.

12. Boys will be Boys

Derek lived on a farm with his parents. He went to a school across the countryside. The long journey to and from school was boring as well as tiring.

One day, Derek decided to take his goat, Joy, along. He had great fun with Joy on the way.

On reaching school, Derek tied Joy under a tree and headed for his class.

Poor Joy, he had never been tied up before. He bleated as loudly as he could, but to no avail. Thirsty and hungry, he started chewing his rope.

Suddenly, Joy was free! He trotted towards Derek's class. He saw Derek seated near a window, put his head inside and nearly chewed off Derek's hair in happiness.

The children rolled with laughter. Even the teacher could not stop laughing.

Derek was embarrassed. He vowed never to take Joy to school again. He decided to travel with his guinea pig the next day!

13. Bobby Young

Once, a kind boy called Bobby Young lived on the edge of Sherwood Forest. He loved the forest and its animals and plants a lot. Each animal was his pet and every blade of grass his friend. He was their friend and protector.

One day, Bobby saw that a gazelle was caught in a trap. He gently freed the creature and tended to its wounds.

Bobby muttered, "I have heard of cruel men who kill animals for fun. I never thought they would strike here. I have to guard my land."

Bobby stayed awake all night, hiding in the bushes for five nights in a row. Finally, he saw the cruel men laying traps in the forest. He quietly followed them home when they finished.

Bobby then ran to the Sheriff's home and told him his story. The Sheriff took his men and caught them. Sherwood Forest was safe again!

14. David and the Dragon

Once, a young boy called David lived in a small town.

One day, David heard that a dragon lived in the Blue Lake, near their town. Thus, in the night, David and his friends went to the lake to see for themselves. Just as they reached the lake, David saw a movement in the still waters. He froze right there in fear! Soon, his friends also saw a huge big shape emerge from the lake.

The three friends turned about and were about to run off when they heard a hoarse yet gentle voice call out, "Boys, please stop! I won't hurt you."

The dragon came close to them and told them that he never hurt people and he lived there all alone. He also made them promise that they would not tell anyone about him.

Thereafter, the boys met the dragon quite often. However, they never told anyone about him ever!

15. The Magic of the Key

Once, there lived a man who was a sergeant in the king's army. The sergeant was a cheerful man, who loved interacting with people.

Once, during a battle, a soldier taught him a few tricks using a key that the soldier always carried in his pocket. The sergeant was very curious! He bought the key from the soldier. While at war, he began practising the tricks and started believing in the magic of the key.

When he returned home, the sergeant started predicting the future of people with his tricks. Once in a party, he predicted 'joy and love' for a young woman. She did not believe him and said she would never love anyone!

After some time, the sergeant's wife fell ill and died soon after. A year later, the sergeant married the young woman, who finally received 'joy and love' as predicted by the magic of the key!

16. Rasmus and John

Once, there lived a boy called Rasmus. His mother worked as a nursemaid at a manor. She was kind and believed in God. His father was a tailor. However, he fell very ill and died.

Rasmus and his mother became poor. Rasmus decided to go on a tour around the world to learn. However, people cheated him and he returned home a very sad person, with no hopes from life. He never tried to improve his life, for he thought no good would come of it.

Then one day, under the willow tree, Rasmus met John. Soon they became friends. John read out psalms for Rasmus. Slowly, Rasmus started believing in the mercy of God.

Quite soon, Rasmus became a cheerful young man. He started working on a farm. He faced problems sometimes, but then he believed that God would help him through them. And so, he was always happy.

17. The Scholar and the Balloon

There was once a man who wanted to fly. However, he did not have a balloon large enough to carry his weight in the sky.

Since he was very learned, he started teaching pupils as a learned scholar. In his spare time, he taught tricks to his flea. He dressed up the flea and taught it how to dance and crack jokes.

Thus, the flea became very popular. Now, the scholar decided to travel the world with the flea and earn money from the tricks. The two visited many countries. Many kings, queens and rich people admired the flea's tricks. All of them rewarded the scholar generously and handsomely. Soon, the scholar made a large amount of money.

The scholar then bought a huge balloon with the money and travelled across the huge sky in it. He was very happy now, as his wish had been fulfilled.

18. The Poor Woman

There once lived a very poor woman. She was very miserable for she had no food to eat. In fact, so poor was she that she had no money to arrange a coffin for her dead husband. She had to bury him without one.

Not a single person would help her and so she shared her grief with the Almighty God, who is ever so kind and giving.

One day, a little canary bird flew into the woman's room from the window. She was surprised to see the bird, as she knew it belonged to her neighbour. She thought they must be looking for it.

Thus, she took the bird back to its owner. The owners were very happy to have their bird back. Impressed by the woman's honesty, they asked her to be their children's caretaker. In return, they would pay her richly.

Thus, the woman lived comfortably.

19. The Penman

In an office, there was a requirement of a person who had a beautiful handwriting for writing official reports. Advertisements were given out in newspapers.

Many people applied for the post and eventually one was selected, who not only had a beautiful handwriting but was also an excellent writer. People would always be impressed when they saw his essays.

However, all the praise made the writer haughty. He wished to become the best writer in the world. Thus, he began writing about other writers and many a times, he would write dreadful things about others.

This behaviour of his angered all other writers. They felt hurt, for the writer wrote bad things about them. One day, they decided to teach him a lesson. They all went to his house and called him names. The writer felt very bad and realised his mistake. Thus, he stopped being vain and hurtful.

20. The Candle at the Ball

One day, a little wax candle was very excited. Their owners had chosen the little candle and his family, to light up a ball that evening. It was the little candle's first ball.

The big father candle instructed them that they should shine brightly. The candles' duty was to give their best light for the ball. The entire family was decorated and set upon silver candlesticks.

The little daughter of the house came dancing into the kitchen. The candles had been placed there. The little girl was excited about staying up late that night. She wanted to wear a new dress for the ball. She twirled about happily.

In the evening, the little candle was shining and gave out a bright glow. The little daughter came wearing her red sash. Her brown eyes shone as brightly as the many candles. It was a day to remember for both – as their first ever ball!

21. The Church Bell

One day, a little boy was very sad. The boy's mother was terribly ill. He loved her dearly. She played with him, and read him stories. The little boy wanted her to recover soon.

The little boy remembered a story his mother had told him. In the story, a little boy had scraped the rust from the church bell so his mother would recover from an illness. He decided he would do the same, hoping his mother would get well.

The boy went to the church in the middle of the night. He climbed up to the bell tower. He was very sacred but scraped the rust from the bell.

The boy came down crying from the bell tower. The minister found him in this condition.

The minister found out why the boy was unhappy. Together, they prayed for the boy's mother. The little boy's mother was better by the morning.

22. Safety in the Snow

Once upon a time, during the war, a small town was under attack from an enemy. It was winter and heavy snowfall made the enemy's progress slow. News of the enemy's arrival reached the town.

Most of the people of the town left, fearing the enemy. One family, who had made the town its home decided to stay, despite the enemy. Their neighbours left in batches throughout the day. The family boarded the windows and prayed through the night. They hid themselves in different parts of the house.

In the morning, afraid of what they might find, they removed the planks from the windows. They were unable to open the door. The house was in complete darkness. The youngest family member crawled out through the loft.

On opening the trap door, they found that it had snowed heavily through the night. The house had been hidden from the enemy's sight. They were saved!

23. Lovely Summers

It was winter, the air was cold and the wind was sharp. A little boy lived with his family on the hill top.

He had planted a tree in his garden that bore beautiful flowers. One day, he went to the tree and said, "When will you be full of lovely flowers?"

The tree said, "You will have to ask the Sun. I will bear lovely flowers the day Sun shines bright on me."

The boy went out and asked the Sun, "Dear Sun, when will your rays fall on my tree?"

The Sun replied, "You will have to ask the snow. My rays will fall on the tree when the snow stops falling."

The boy went to the snow and prayed, "Please stop falling and let the Sun shine."

After the few days, the snow stopped falling and the Sun started shining. Soon the tree was full of lovely purple flowers.

24. The Silver Coin

Once, a man kept a silver coin in his wallet and never spent it. He believed that the coin was very lucky for him.

However, the coin wanted to travel the world. One day, it said, "Why have you kept me in this dirty wallet since ages? Give me to somebody else and let me be free."

Finally, the man gave the coin in return of some money. Now, the coin moved from one wallet to the other.

One girl wore it in her neck. After a few days it fell off her neck, on the floor. Nobody took care of it. It prayed hard to find his master.

Suddenly, it found itself in the hands of the man. It said, "I have travelled the entire world, but the safest place is your wallet. Please put me back in it."

The man was also delighted to have his coin back.

25. The Haughty Hermit

Once, in a village there lived a learned but proud hermit.

One day, a man went to meet the hermit. The haughty hermit did not come to meet the man.

Just then, a student of the hermit went to him with a message. "Sir, the prince is here to see you," the student said. "I will go and meet him," said the hermit.

The prince talked to the hermit and left. The man then walked up to the hermit and said, "You did not greet me when I came to meet you, but you welcomed the king's son quite readily. Why?"

The hermit replied cleverly, "For me, greeting means not greeting and not greeting means greeting."

Hearing this, the man hit him hard with his stick. The hermit screamed, "Why did you hit me?"

To this, the man replied, "For me beating means not beating and not beating means beating."

26. The Saint and the Young Man

Once, a young man felt very sad in the city. So, he decided to live in a forest. After some time he reached a quiet place but a saint already lived there in his hut.

The young man requested the saint to let him stay there for a while. The saint agreed.

After a few days, the saint saw the young man cutting the branches of a tree. He asked, "Why are you hurting the poor tree?"

The young man replied, "These branches are not required and take a lot of space." After some days, the young man cut a few trees and bushes.

The saint shouted, "You have come from the city and have no love for Mother Nature. You have no right to destroy God's creations. If I let you stay any longer, you will ruin the entire forest… so please leave!"

The young man was ashamed and left the forest.

27. The Angel's Challenge

Once, God had a meeting with his angels. God had divided power among all his angels. He wanted to check if the angels respected the power they were given.

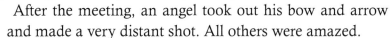

After the meeting, an angel took out his bow and arrow and made a very distant shot. All others were amazed.

He became proud and said, "No one can shoot as far as I can."

The other angels said, "Don't be so proud. God can shoot better."

The proud angel challenged God. God accepted his challenge. The angel shot. God smiled and covered the entire universe in one single step. Everybody was amazed.

Now, there was no space left to make a shot. God said, "I have covered the entire universe one step. It is hundred times the distance you covered in one shot. Do you still doubt my strength and power?"

The angel was ashamed and apologised to God.

28. The Farmer and the Merchant

There was once a farmer who lived in a tiny cottage. He had built it with his own hands.

His neighbour was a merchant, who had a large house and a lot of money. He also had many people who worked for him.

The merchant would always make fun of the farmer, "You poor man! You have to do all your work yourself. No wonder your clothes are always dirty."

One day, a thunderstorm blew away the roofs of all the houses. All the roads were flooded.

The merchant had nothing to eat in his house. His house was without a roof. The farmer repaired his own roof and gave the merchant some vegetables.

He said, "Sir, I may have a small house and work day and night. But, I know how to put a roof on my house and grow my own food. My labour saved me today."

29. The Man in Love

Once upon a time, there was a castle. However, the castle was ancient, and its walls were weak. Soon the castle would fall.

Therefore, its residents decided to leave. However, the man in love did not leave it, for his beloved was buried in the castle.

Soon, the walls of the castle began to fall. The man in love was frightened. He called out to a vain lady. She replied, "You are covered with dust! You will ruin my beautiful carriage."

The man in love then asked the sad boy to help him. He said, "Oh, I am so sad. I do not want company right now!"

Then, Old Father Time came and saved the man in love. He was very thankful. He asked a knowledgeable fellow, "Why did Old Father Time save me, when nobody else did?"

The knowledgeable fellow smiled, "Because only Old Father Time knows how valuable love is."

30. The Unfaithful Fortune

Once upon a time, there lived two friends in a village. One day, one friend said to the other, "Dear Friend, fortune does not favour those who wait for it. Let us go and seek our fortunes."

"I don't think we have a better destiny than the present," said the other friend, "You may go ahead with your search, though. I know you will come back disappointed."

The ambitious friend went places looking for fortune. He undertook adventures, faced dangers, but in vain. He was tired. Everyone told him that fortune was unfaithful. One must not run after it.

The ambitious friend realised his mistake and came back to his village. He was very happy to reach his peaceful village and decided never to leave the place again. He went to see his old friend. He saw that his friend had done well and was living a happy life.

31. The Two Friends

Once, there lived two friends. They started a business together. They worked very hard in the beginning. Unfortunately, the business was unsuccessful and the two friends had to suffer a big loss.

So they decided to close the business.

Both the friends blamed each other and fought. They started calling each other names. They were so angry with each other that each was prepared to kill the other.

One day, one of them set the other friend's house on fire. When that friend returned and saw his house in ashes, he was very angry. He at once set the first friend's house on fire to take revenge.

After a few months, one of them approached the other and said, "Let's stop this madness and be friends like before."

"True," said the other. "We should not suffer loss of friendship for loss of money."

Thus, the two forgave each other.

1. Young Mouse, the Cock and the Cat

Once, a young mouse lived with his mother. His mother always told him not to go out alone.

One day, the naughty young mouse went out of the hole. He returned home and said, "O Mother! I visited many places. I remember two creatures I saw. The first one was large and had ugly feet. He had red flesh on his head and on his chin. His voice was very loud. However, the other creature I saw was very pretty. She was also large and had a shiny coat of fur. Her eyes were green and beautiful. Her voice was very soft."

His mother replied, "The first creature you call ugly is a cock. Humans will kill him and throw away his bones. Then, we shall have a hearty meal of his bones. The other creature you call beautiful is a cat. She will eat us the first chance she gets."

2. The Jumper

Once, there was a city in the mountains, called Hope Land. The king of Hope Land wanted to find a match for his daughter, the princess. Thus, he invited all the suitors to his palace and said, "Whoever jumps the highest will be married to my daughter, for he will be the bravest man of Hope Land."

Many suitors came forward to win the hand of the beautiful princess. However, no one could jump high. In the end, three suitors entered the palace - a flea, a grasshopper and Jack, the toy.

First, the flea came forward. He said, "I have royal blood in my veins. I have good manners, and so I am fit to marry the princess and become the future king!" Then, he jumped. He rose a few feet in the air but, at that moment, the chambermaid waved the king's fan. The wind from the fan blew the flea away!

Next, the grasshopper came forward. He said, "I belong to an ancient Egyptian family. We are well-mannered, learned and royal. Thus, I should get the princess' hand." Then, he jumped. However, his foot slipped as he jumped and he fell on the king's face.

This made the king very angry. He ordered his guards to throw the grasshopper out of the palace.

Now it was Jack, the toy's turn. He did not say anything, but prepared to jump. He jumped very high, and then landed straight in front of the princess.

The king was very happy now. He said, "Jack the toy did not talk like the flea and the grasshopper, but jumped the highest. He does not boast about himself, but believes in his work. He shall marry my daughter!"

Soon, Jack, the toy was married to the princess, and they lived happily.

3. The Clever Geese

One day, a fox went to a meadow. A farmer had left his geese there and was resting under a nearby tree.

The fox saw the geese and shouted happily, "Oh good! I will eat these geese one after the other."

The geese saw him and cackled with terror. However, just as the fox was about to pounce on the closest goose, one of them said, "Oh mighty fox, before you kill us, please grant our last wish. Let us pray to God."

The fox thought and said, "Okay then, pray! I will wait till you are done."

The first goose began a very long prayer. The second goose joined in, followed by the third and the fourth. Soon, they were all cackling aloud together.

The owner of the geese heard their cry and came running. He drove the fox away with a huge stick!

Thus, the clever geese were saved.

4. The Spinner

Once, a spinner lived with his lazy wife. She would always be angry with him.

The poor spinner worked all day making yarn. Then at night, he would cook dinner, as his wife would refuse to do any work. But he would never complain.

One day, the poor spinner fell very ill. The spinner's wife was worried. She rushed to bring the doctor.

The doctor checked the spinner and said, "He has very high fever. Please take care of him or he will die."

The spinner's wife was very sad. She thought, "Oh! He is such a kind and good man! I always shouted at him, but he never said an unkind word to me ever. Now, I will do my best to save him."

Thus, she started taking good care of him and he became better in a few days. From then on, the spinner's wife did all her work, cheerfully!

5. The Fox and the Horse

Once, a peasant had a horse, which had grown old. The peasant said, "Go away! You are of no use to me. But, if you prove your strength by bringing me a lion, I will feed you."

The horse sadly went to the forest. There, he met a fox and told him his story. The fox said, "I will help you. Just lie down as if you were dead."

The fox then went to the lion and said, "A dead horse is lying outside. I will fasten the horse's tail to yours, and you can drag it into your cave."

When the fox had tied the tails, he shouted, "Pull!" The horse sprang up and dragged the lion to the peasant's house.

The peasant was shocked to see the lion. He realised his mistake and said to the horse, "I will take care of you as long as you live.

6. Doctor Knowall

Once, a farmer named Crabb wanted to be a doctor.

The local doctor suggested, "Crabb, put up a sign on your door that says 'Dr. Knowall'."

One day, some thieves stole some gold from a rich lord's house. Worried, he called Crabb for dinner. At dinner, when a servant brought the first dish, Crabb said to the rich lord, "This is the first." The servant was frightened because he was the first thief.

The same happened to the second and the third servant who were also thieves. The fourth servant brought a dish of crabs that was covered. The lord asked Crabb to guess the dish. Crabb didn't know and cried, "Poor Crabb!"

The lord cried, "He knows everything!"

The servants took Crabb aside and confessed everything. Then Crabb showed the lord where the gold was, but didn't name the thieves. He received rewards from both sides and became a renowned man.

7. Gambling Hansel

Once, there lived a gambler named Hansel. One day, God came to his house at night and requested for shelter. In the morning, God said, "Hansel, ask me for three boons."

Hansel replied, "Give me a pack of cards and a dice with which I can win everything. Also, give me a tree from which no one can descend without my permission." God granted his wishes.

Then on, Hansel started winning everything with his cards and dice. So, St. Peter sent Death to Hansel. Hansel tricked Death into climbing the tree. After seven years, the Lord commanded Hansel to let Death come down.

Death took Hansel to Hell. Hansel won over the Devil in Hell and started poking Heaven. St. Peter had to let him enter.

But when Hansel started gambling in Heaven, St. Peter threw him out.

Hansel's soul broke into pieces and entered the gambling vagabonds of today.

8. Old Hildebrand

Once, there lived a kind peasant named Hildebrand.

The village grocer was a greedy man. He wanted Hildebrand's farm. So, one day, he told Hildebrand, "Brother, some laurel-leaves grow on the Gockerli Hill in Italy. If you get them, it will cure sick people at once."

Hildebrand wanted to help many ill people in his village, thus he set out immediately.

However, on his way, he met an egg-merchant who said, "The grocer is trying to fool you. Come with me and I will show you."

The egg-merchant hid Hildebrand in his huge basket and went to his farm. There, they heard the grocer singing with his wife.

The grocer's wife sang, "You have sent Hildebrand away to the Gockerli Hill." The grocer joined in, "I will sell his farm off before he comes back."

Hildebrand immediately climbed out of the basket, and chased the evil grocer and his wife away.

9. The Sorcerer

One day, a sorcerer was showing magic to a crowd. He made a cock lift a heavy beam and walk.

There was also a wise boy in the crowd. He saw that the beam was actually a straw. He shouted, "The cock is carrying a straw, not a beam!"

Immediately, the magic vanished. Everyone saw the straw, and drove the sorcerer away. The sorcerer was very angry. He wanted revenge.

Soon, the boy's birthday came. On his way to the church, he had to cross a stream. So, he took off his shoes and started walking in the water.

Suddenly, the sorcerer appeared and tried to push him towards the deep water. But the boy was very strong; he pushed the sorcerer backwards. He also kept praying to God.

Quite soon, the sorcerer himself fell into the water and drowned. The boy knew that God had helped him.

10. The Dream of Paris

Once, an old teacher taught history to little children under an oak tree.

The village children listened attentively as the teacher told them about France. He spoke of the shepherd girl, Joan of Arc, Charlotte Corday, Henry the Fourth and Napoleon the First.

The children would dream of going to Paris one day. But the teacher warned everyone, "Don't go to Paris! If you go there, you will be ruined."

Even then, they couldn't stop imagining about Paris. Among the children, there was a little ragged boy called Tom. He drew lovely pictures. One day, Tom did go to Paris - the great city and started living there.

After many years, Tom returned to the village. The teacher recognised him and said, "So you went to Paris after all. It ruined you, poor Tom!"

But contrary to his teacher's thoughts, Tom had done well and had become a famous artist in Paris.

11. Hercules and Quarrel

Once, Hercules was travelling along a road. On his way, he met a strange creature. He came close to Hercules and was about to hit him. At once, Hercules beat him with his club.

Hercules thought that the creature was beaten and dead. Thus, he began walking again. However, the creature came again and stood before him. Hercules was surprised because now the creature had doubled in size and looked dangerous. Thus, Hercules beat him again with his club. The creature grew in size again.

The more Hercules hit the creature, the more it grew in size. The creature became so large that it filled the entire road where Hercules walked.

Suddenly, God Pallas appeared before Hercules and said, "O Hercules! Stop hitting this ugly creature. Its name is Quarrel and he will grow larger each time you beat it. Leave it alone, and it will be small again."

12. The Punishment

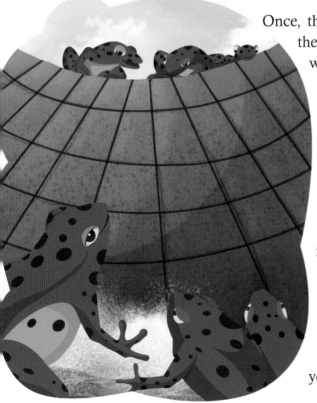

Once, there was a deep well. A family of frogs lived there. One day, a family of toads came to visit the well. The frogs allowed them to stay in the well.

The newcomers liked the well so much that they were determined never to leave the well. When the frogs eventually discovered these intentions, they were angry but they could do nothing about it.

One day, mother-toad got into a bucket, which was being used to pull the water out. She kept going up and up till it became too bright for her. She quickly jumped back into the water. But, she fell with a terrible flop and died!

The toads were scared that they would all be killed! Thus, they left the well the next day.

Mother-frog taught her young ones, "Never snatch or steal someone else's things slyly, or you will be punished like mother-toad was!"

13. Tit for Tat

Once, two friends, Ronny and Mike, went camping in the Redwood Forest. They set up their tent at a pretty location and cooked food. Tired after a hard day's work, they went to a nearby stream and enjoyed a long wash.

However, when they returned, someone had stolen their things and eaten their food.

Ronny was very angry but Mike said, "Don't worry! We will be prepared when they come next."

The next morning, the two boys filled two buckets with water and dirt. Each climbed a tree on either side of the path and hid themselves there. They did not have to wait long! They saw some boys approaching them and got ready.

Ronny and Mike tipped the buckets over the boys as soon as they came under the tree. Startled, the boys ran off screaming!

Then, Ronny and Mike spent the rest of their camping happily.

14. The Ass and His Master

Once, there was a hard-working ass. But his master did not treat him well.

One day, his master loaded him with a huge load of earthenware.

The ass did not have much strength. The road on which he had to carry the load was uneven and rough. This was very difficult for the ass. He kept slipping many times.

Suddenly, the ass lost his balance and fell down on the ground. All the earthen vessels broke into many pieces.

His master was very angry, as now he would not be able to earn any money. He began to beat the ass without any pity.

The ass, feeling much pain in his heart and body, lifted his head from the ground and sternly said, "You selfish, greedy and cruel man. You first starve me by giving little food, and then load me with more than I can carry; you deserve this bad luck because of your injustice to me."

15. The Naughty Boy

Once, there was a naughty boy. He lived in a village through which a river flowed.

The boy's mother had warned him, "Do not go to the river, it is dangerous for a little boy like you. You don't know how to swim."

One summer's day, when his mother was taking a nap, the boy slipped out of his house.

The boy went to the river. There he saw many big boys playing in the water and bathing. He too wanted to enjoy in the water. Soon he dipped himself in the river and started bathing.

However, he did not know how to swim and started drowning. Scared, he shouted out for help!

Some boys pulled him out at once. They said, "You careless boy! Why did you get into the river if you did not know how to swim?"

The boy was very ashamed and never disobeyed his mother again!

16. Bobby Dagger

Once, there lived a sea pirate called Bobby Dagger. He travelled the seas with his buddies, Storm and Hail, looting ships.

The three had amassed a rather huge treasure. However, Dagger was now growing old. He was ashamed of his bad ways.

Thus, one day, Dagger called his buddies and said, "I have buried the treasure under an oak tree at the old age home. You can share it after I die."

After a few days, Dagger died. Storm and Hail went to the place he had described. To their dismay, there were lots of oak trees in the garden. They started digging. At last, they found a large metal box. Inside they found a message.

It said, 'Leave your bad ways and stay here. You will have a good life.'

Storm and Hail realised that Dagger had wanted to guide them to the right path. They became good people and lived happily.

17. The Lord's Animals and the Devil's

Long ago, God created all animals, and the Devil created goats.

The long tails of goats got stuck everywhere. So, the Devil bit off their tails.

The goats destroyed plants and vines. So, the God's wolves killed the goats. The angry Devil complained to God.

God answered, "Why did you create harmful creatures?" Devil said, "It's my nature to do evil! You must pay me for the goats."

God agreed to pay him as soon as the oak-leaves fell. When the oak-leaves fell, Devil went to God. But God said, "The leaves of the oak-tree at Constantinople have not fallen."

The Devil searched for six months and found that oak-tree. But by then, all the oaks had leaves again.

The angry Devil pulled out the eyes of all his remaining goats, and put his own instead. That's why goats have Devil's eyes and short tails!

18. A Special Boy

Once, there lived a young boy. The boy had a special gift. He could understand the language of dogs and could talk to them.

One day, the boy came to know that far away in a kingdom, the people were being troubled by a pack of dogs that ate little children at night. The king had declared a huge reward for anyone who could solve the problem.

The boy at once set off for the kingdom, where he met the king. After listening to the lad, the king asked his men to escort the boy to the place where the dogs hovered.

After sometime, the boy returned to the palace and informed the king that the dogs were under a spell. They were guarding a treasure, which was buried in the forest.

The hidden treasure was taken out and distributed among the people. The dogs mysteriously disappeared and never returned.

19. The Old Hut

Once, there lived a lady, who was a fortune-teller. She lived in a small hut. She told people their future in exchange of gold.

The lady used all kinds of tricks to convince people. People believed whatever she told them. Soon, she became famous and rich. She bought a new house and rented out her old hut to another poor woman.

Out of habit, people continued to go to the old hut. The new lady told them that she was not a fortune-teller. However, people did not believe her. She had no option but to tell people what they wanted to hear from her. Thus, many people started to come to her.

Thereafter, the lady who first lived there became poor, because no one went to her now.

Thus, the old hut changed the fate of its new mistress and the old mistress lost her trade.

20. The Sunbeam and the Prisoner

Once, a prisoner was being taken across the country in a ship. He was locked up in a dark room that didn't even have a window. It just had a tiny opening through which the prisoner could see a little bit of the outside view.

The poor prisoner was very lonely and sad. Just then, he noticed a sunbeam seeping in through a tiny opening in the cabin wall. Then, a little bird flew up to the opening and sang beautifully.

The prisoner walked up to the opening and saw numerous ships sailing in the sea and trees swaying on the island. They all had freedom but he was a captive! He felt sorry for his misdeeds.

This also made the prisoner realise that no matter how bad the condition, there is always a hope of sunshine in everyone's life. One must never lose hope, as life is the most beautiful gift bestowed upon us by the Almighty.

21. The Black Spots

Once, there was an ancient city called Golden City. The people of Golden City had a black spot on their chests. Each person's black spot was filled with others' faults.

Once, the people of Golden City began to quarrel. They said to each other, "My black spot is large now! You have so many faults!"

When the builder of Golden City came to meet them, they complained to him.

The builder placed a huge mirror before them and said, "Stand with your backs to this mirror. Turn your neck and look at yourselves in the mirror."

To their surprise, each person had a large black spot on his back. The builder said, "The black spot on your back is filled with your own faults. It is large, too. All of you only saw the faults of others, and did not notice your own faults!"

The people of Golden City stopped fighting.

22. Ulysses and his Friends

Once, Ulysses set off on a ship to sea with his servants. Soon, he reached the island ruled by Circe, Apollo's daughter. Circe offered the men a delicious drink, which turned them into animals. However, Ulysses turned away the dangerous drink.

Instead, he offered Circe a magical drink. She drank it and fell in love with him. Ulysses asked Circe to turn his servants into men again.

Circe agreed and said, "Animals, do you want to change?"

The Lion roared, "I am not a fool to give up my royal status. Why should I wish for a change?"

The Beer grunted, "We are happy as we are free from all worries and troubles. We do not intend to change."

"A man is no better than me," said the Wolf, "I would rather be a Wolf than a Man."

Ulysses realised that animals lived a happier life. They also lived together peacefully!

23. The Magic Paintbrush

Once, there lived a poor boy. His parents died in an accident and there was no one to look after him.

The boy often sat on the seashore and drew on sand. This way, the boy grew to be a good artist.

One day, the boy found a magic paintbrush. Anything he painted turned into reality! Thus, he helped people with food and clothes.

One day, the king heard about the magic paintbrush and the painter. He asked him to paint an island of gold.

So, the painter painted a sea and an island in gold in the middle. As soon as the painting was complete, it turned real.

The king started sailing towards the golden island. Then, the painter painted a deadly storm in the sea. The king drowned in the storm and died. The painter felt very bad and he threw the paintbrush in the sea.

24. The King and the Deer

Once, a king went hunting. After a long wait, the king saw a deer and ran after him. The deer was swift and so he quickly ran away.

The poor king was tired of running and decided to stop. Suddenly, he fell into a pit made by a hunter to trap animals. The king started shouting, "Oh! Someone, please help me!"

The deer heard the king's cry and turned back to see what the trouble was.

When the deer saw the king in the pit, he felt sorry for him. Thus, he caught hold of a huge rock with his hind legs and went down into the pit. The king held on to the deer's neck and tried to climb the wall of the pit. After, much struggle, the king was up and saved.

The king felt ashamed that the same deer, whom he had wanted to kill, saved him.

25. The Washerman's Donkey

Once, there lived a washerman in a certain city. One night, when he was fast asleep, a thief got into the house. In a corner of the washermans' courtyard, was a donkey tied with a rope, while his dog sat nearby.

When the donkey saw the thief enter the house, he said to the dog, "Surely it's your duty to wake up the master!"

"Don't tell me about my duties!" snapped the dog. "You know very well that I've been guarding this house for a long time. He has not fed me well lately, so I don't care what happens to him."

The concerned donkey decided to wake up the master and brayed loudly. The master woke up and saw the thief. He hit the thief till he ran away.

Then, he thanked the donkey for helping him. Thereafter, he took good care of the donkey.

26. The Foolish Son's Bravery

Once, there lived a rich man, who had a son. The son was very foolish and could not learn anything. The rich man sent him to three different masters for a year. When he came back, the boy's father asked him what he had learnt.

The boy said, "I have learnt the language of the dogs, the frogs and the birds." Hearing this, the rich man was very angry and told his son to leave his house.

The boy left home and went to another kingdom. There, a witch had kidnapped the baby prince. The boy at once offered his help in finding the prince. The brave boy went alone into the jungle. With the help of his knowledge of talking to animals; he found where the baby prince was and saved him. The king rewarded the boy for his bravery and appointed him as a minister in the court.

27. The Loyal Dog

Once, a man brought a dog and named him Oscar. However, the man's wife did not like Oscar.

Oscar's master trained him to bring his midday meal from home.

One day, the master's wife made mutton for her husband. She hung the lunch box around Oscar's neck and sent him to the fields.

On the way, Oscar met a bigger dog. The bigger dog asked Oscar for the meat but Oscar refused.

The bigger dog tried to snatch the box from him. They fought and Oscar was injured.

The master's friend saw the two dogs fighting and recognised Oscar. He hit the bigger dog with a stick and drove him away.

Now, he carried the dog to his master and told him the entire story. The master had tears in his eyes. He bandaged the dog and took him home. The master's wife was ashamed and praised the dog for his loyalty.

28. The Crows and the Rooster

Once, a farmer lived with his wife on a beautiful farm. Early one morning, some crows flew to the field and started eating the ripe corn.

The old rooster began to crow excitedly, "Wake up, wake up!" The farmer's wife woke up and said, "The rooster is crowing, let us go and check!"

The farmer said lazily, "That's just the old rooster. I am certain there is nothing wrong!" Thus, the farmer and his wife kept sleeping and the crows kept eating.

Soon, the sun rose brightly and the farmer and his wife finally woke up. When they went to their field, they found that the corn was all gone.

The farmer said, "Oh what will I do now? All my hard work has gone to waste!"

His wife said, "We were careless. The old rooster crowed so loudly. We should have got up to see what the matter was!"

29. The Fishermen

Every morning, the fishermen went to the sea to catch fish and other sea animals. Then they would sell them in the market and earn money.

One day, the fishermen went to the sea with their big net. They threw the net in the water. When it was time to pull up the net, they all became very happy as it was very heavy. As they pulled the net, they were all very disappointed. The net was full of sand and stones and the fish were very few. It was not what they had expected.

An old and wise fisherman said, "We should all stop crying about it. The truth is that sorrow is the sister of happiness. At one moment we were very happy and the next moment we were sad. If we accept the joys of life, we should suffer the pain also. We should learn from it."

30. The Cat and the Canary

Once, there were two brothers, Raymond and Edward. Both of them had a pet each. Raymond had a cat and Edward a canary. Surprisingly, the cat and the canary were also good friends. However, Edward never trusted the cat.

One day, Edward was playing in a park near their house. Suddenly, he saw the cat running towards him followed by Tim, his little brother. The cat had the canary in his mouth. Edward was upset and angry.

He thought, 'Oh! The cat ate my canary!'

Edward picked up a stick and hit the cat hard on its head.

"What have you done?" exclaimed Tim. "The canary was hurt, that's why the cat carried it to you."

Edward was ashamed. He thought, "I should have trusted the cat."

Edward took care of both the cat and the canary. He promised himself that, henceforth, he would always think before reacting to anything.

1. Ludwig's Magic Potion

Ludwig was a poor soldier. He was travelling through the countryside. One day, in a forest, Ludwig met another soldier. They decided to travel together.

Ludwig and his friend wandered through many villages in search of food. One day, they reached a farmer's hut. Everybody was sad in the house because the farmer was very sick.

Ludwig's friend said to him, "Friend, you have a magic potion with you. One drop of the potion could cure any disease. Why don't you give the farmer the magic potion?"

Ludwig offered to help the farmer's family. The wife was desperate for her husband to recover and agreed.

Ludwig went to the farmer. He put a drop of the potion in the farmer's mouth. The farmer was well again.

The grateful farmer offered Ludwig a lamb as a reward. Thanks to the magic potion, Ludwig and his friend did not go hungry again.

2. Foolish Hans

Once, there lived a man called Hans. One day, his wife Gretel said, "Hans, my mother is coming to our house for supper tonight. Please take a paper bag, a jute bag and a glass bottle to the market place. Buy some olives and put them in this paper bag. Then, buy some ice and put it in the jute bag. Finally, buy some honey and put it in this bottle."

Hans went to the market place. The vegetable shop's owner said, "Sir, I do not have olives, but I have olive juice!" Thus, Hans bought olive juice and put it in the paper bag.

Next, Hans went to buy ice. The shopkeeper said, "Sir, I do not have ice, but I have cold water!" Hans bought cold water and put it in the jute bag.

Now, Hans went to buy honey. The shopkeeper said, "Sir, I do not have honey, but I have a beehive that you can take!" Hans bought a beehive, but as he tried to stuff the beehive in the glass bottle, the angry honeybees stung him on his face and hands.

Stung and crying, Hans reached home. Gretel said, "Oh, Hans! What happened to you? The paper bag, the jute bag and the bottle are all empty!"

Hans told Gretel about the events of the market place. Gretel said, "Foolish Hans! You put juice in the paper bag, and it leaked! You put water in the jute bag, and that leaked too! You should never meddle with a beehive that is why the bees stung you! Now you are hurt. All your money is wasted and you returned from the market empty handed!"

Hans said, "You are right. Now I will always use my mind, not just follow instructions, blindly."

3. The Camel

Once, a young man was lost in a faraway desert. He was tired of walking. Just then, he saw a camel for the first time. He thought, "This animal looks scary. He has long legs, curved neck and a big hump!"

However, after some time, he noticed that the camel had not attacked him. Nor had he made any roaring noise. The young man thought, "This animal is a little different from the wild ones. Let me see if I can ride it."

The young man approached the camel but the camel still did not scare him. He was surprised, "This animal seems to be a gentle one. Let me go closer and try and pat him."

The young man went closer to the camel and touched his body. The camel did not respond. The young man rode the camel happily!

Thereafter, men started using camels for travelling across deserts.

4. The Prince in the Fairyland

One day, a prince went to the forest for hunting. There, he caught a golden deer. The golden deer spoke, "Prince, do not kill me! I will give you something better." The prince agreed and they set out. After two days of flying, the deer landed in a new land and said, "You are in Fairyland. I am actually a fairy prince. Thank you for sparing my life. Come with me to my palace."

The prince visited the palace. There, he saw a magnificent garden, which had a beautiful golden swing. He decided to rest there.

Since he was tired, the prince fell asleep. While he slept, a fairy princess flew down in the form of a white pigeon. She saw the prince, and at once, fell in love with him. The prince woke up and decided to head back home. The fairy prince gave him the white pigeon as a gift. Once the prince reached home, the pigeon turned into the fairy princess! The prince fell in love with the beautiful princess. Soon, they were married and lived happily ever after.

5. Spellbound

Once, a lady set out to free her husband who was under the spell of an evil witch. The evil witch had transformed him into a mouse and was holding him captive in her castle.

The lady did not know the location of the witch's castle. She asked the Sun for directions to the castle. The Sun could not help her, but gave her a basket to use whenever she was in trouble. The basket contained a magic carpet that could take a person anywhere.

The lady then asked the Moon to help her. The Moon gave her a magic cloak and sent her to the wind.

The wind told her the location of the castle and gave her a magic potion to transform her husband. The lady reached the castle in the magic cloak. She gave her husband the magic potion and they flew back home on the carpet.

6. The Talking Horse

Once, there lived a beautiful princess. She set out on a journey to marry a prince from a neighbouring kingdom. Her maid and her horse accompanied the princess. This horse was a talking horse and was extremely loyal to the princess.

While in the forest, the maid imprisoned the princess and dressed as the princess herself. The maid made the princess promise not to reveal her true identity.

The talking horse saw all that happened, but it kept quiet fearing for the princess' life. Now, the maid did not know that the horse could talk. She was sure that her plan to marry the prince would succeed.

They reached the prince's kingdom. Everyone thought that the maid was the princess. But the talking horse told the prince the truth. The princess was recognised by her royal seal. The prince and princess were married. The wicked maid was punished.

7. The Giant's Wages

Once, there lived a giant. He decided to leave home and travel the world. Before leaving, he asked his father for an iron staff. His father brought him a staff, but the giant broke it with a single snap. He understood that the ironsmith was cheating people.

The giant went to the ironsmith. The smith agreed to hire the strong giant. The giant did not want any wages. Instead, he would give the smith's iron two hefty blows. Being a greedy man, the smith agreed.

The giant began work the next day. He struck the iron with a mighty blow. With one blow the iron was buried deep in the ground. This angered the smith. He asked the giant to leave.

The giant gave the smith a blow. Then, he took the iron, which was buried in the ground and left.

The smith never cheated people again.

8. The Seven Dwarves

Once, seven little dwarves decided to travel. They all walked in a row. One day, an insect flew by them buzzing. One of the dwarves jumped over a hedge in fright. The others thought some enemy had attacked and yelled, "We surrender!"

When they did not see anyone around, they journeyed forward.

Then, they saw a sleeping hare and mistook it to be a dragon. After a long discussion, they decided to attack the hare. But, as they were running towards the hare, it ran away.

The dwarves continued their journey and came to a deep river. They asked a man on the opposite side of the river how to get across. He could not hear them and yelled, "What?" They mistook it as "Wade."

So, they started to wade into the river. The kind man saved them and said, "Dwarves, unless you grow up, stay home and learn your lessons!"

9. The Three Young Men

Once, three young men went looking for work. On their way, they met the Devil. He said, "If you do as I say, you will always be rich. One of you will say, 'All three of us,' the second 'For money,' and the third, 'And quite right, too'." He then told them to go to a certain inn.

At midnight, the three young men saw the inn-keeper kill a rich merchant for his gold. The next morning, the police came and asked, "Who killed the merchant?"

"All three of us," said the first.

"For money," said the second.

The third added, "And quite right, too."

The judge sentenced them to death. Just then, the Devil appeared and said, "You may now speak." They told the truth and the inn-keeper was executed.

Devil said, "I have the inn-keeper's evil soul. You three are now free, and will always be rich."

10. The Honest Servant

Once, a rich miser had an honest servant.

Once, the servant decided to travel. On his way, he met a poor dwarf and gave him his money. The grateful dwarf granted him three boons - a gun that never missed its target, a fiddle that made everyone dance and the power of getting all his requests accepted.

The servant returned home. And the evil miser took away all his gifts. Then, he killed a rich man with the gun and stole his money. The servant kept quiet.

However, the miser went to the judge and told him that his servant had robbed the rich man and killed him. So, the servant was sentenced to death. But he said, "Please let me play my fiddle one last time."

The miser had to get the fiddle. The servant played and everyone started dancing. He wouldn't stop till the miser finally confessed! Finally the judge acquitted the servant and punished the miser.

11. The Three Army-Surgeons

Once, three army-surgeons were boasting before an inn-keeper. The first said that he could cut off his hand, and join it back. The second said he could tear out his heart, and replace it. The third said he could gouge out his eyes and heal them. Then, they cut those organs and put them on a plate.

The inn-keeper's servant-girl put the plate in the cupboard. But, a cat came and ate the organs. So, she replaced them with a thief's hand, a cat's eyes and a pig's heart. In the morning, the surgeons put the organs back in their bodies.

On their way, the first surgeon kept behaving like a pig, the second could not see and the third kept snatching people's money. They realised that something was wrong. So, they went to the inn-keeper. When they got to know the truth, they felt sorry for their careless behaviour.

12. Thomas and Mary

Once, a boy called Thomas lived in a small cottage with his parents. At the end of the same lane lived a very famous singer. He had a very pretty daughter called Mary.

When she was little, Mary used to go to the park to play. Thomas was not allowed to go to the park since he was poor. So, he would sit outside the park and paint. He would often gift his paintings to Mary.

Thomas then went on to study and became a professional painter. He once visited a czar's palace. He liked it so much, that he painted the palace. But, he also labelled certain parts as "Here Mary sleeps", "Here Mary dances," and sent these painting to Mary.

After many years, Thomas became rich. Then, he married Mary and built exactly the same palace for her as he had painted in his picture.

13. Teapot

Once, there lived a rich lady who was fond of collecting expensive chinaware. Her favourite was a blue teapot that had a lovely shape.

The lady took the pot out, only for special parties. The guests always appreciated it.

Soon, the teapot became proud. One day, it was lying inside the cupboard with the other crockery. It said, "I am the most beautiful of all crockery and should not be kept in the same dirty cupboard as you all. I want to be placed in a new cupboard with exclusive silverware."

The others were very hurt but the teapot did not care.

One day, the lady took it out to clean it for a party. It fell off her hand and its handle broke. Now, it was useless for the lady.

She kept it in the store amongst other useless things. The teapot cried and said, "God has punished me for being proud."

14. The Boy and Jesus Christ

Once, a boy lived with his parents. His parents wanted him to go to church every Sunday but he refused.

The boy liked sleeping till late on Sundays. One day, his father said, "If you don't come to church with us, Christ will not listen to your prayers."

The boy asked his father, "Who is Christ and how did he die?"

The father replied, "Jesus Christ is our God. He came on earth to teach mankind to love each other and live in harmony. Many people became jealous of his growing popularity and cruelly killed him. He was hung on a cross with nails."

The boy had tears in his eyes. The father further said, "We must always remember what he preached and live accordingly. This is the reason I insist that you go to church."

The boy understood and never refused to go to the church again.

15. Life's Lessons

Once, a young man requested a trainer to teach him the art of sword fighting.

The trainer agreed. Now, the young man started living in the trainer's house.

The next day onwards, the trainer made the young man get up early in the morning. He then made him do all the daily chores like washing, cleaning and cooking. Later in the afternoon, the young man would take the trainer's sheep to graze. Then in the evening he would chop wood for the fire.

One day, the young man got fed up and said, "I have come here to learn and not do household work. Kindly begin my lessons."

The trainer laughed and said, "Young man, these are life's lessons. You have learned to live independently. Also, you have developed the stamina to face any circumstances in life."

The young man understood and thanked his trainer for the lessons.

16. The Kind Boy

Once, there was a boy who lived in a village. Everyone liked him because he was very helpful and caring.

One day, when he was going to school, he saw an old woman crossing the road. He went to help the woman but, while doing so, he fell on a pile of logs and broke his ankle.

The doctor plastered his ankle and advised him six weeks' rest. He was very sad because he could not go to school, and he had to appear for his examinations the next month.

The boy asked his best friend to come to his house and explain the lessons, but his friend refused saying that he had to study himself. He asked his other friends but they too gave some excuse. At last, his teachers helped him in preparing for the examination.

The boy scored the highest in his class and was praised by all.

17. The Determined Boy

Once, there lived a little boy in a poor family. He did odd jobs like collecting rags, instead of going to school, as he had no money.

The boy wanted to play with the rich boys, get good education but his parents stopped him. One day, he saw how an ant, which was trapped in a web, escaped. The boy learnt that everything was possible with hard work and dedication.

One fine day, he saw a group of rich boys come to the forest to practice archery with their master. The boy approached the master and requested him to teach him archery. But, the master refused for he did not teach poor people.

The boy now made a statue of the master, and practised archery every day in front of it. Slowly, he became a very good archer. Thus, with constant perseverance and dedication, the boy achieved what he wanted in life.

18. The Brave Puppy

Once, there was a boy called Jack who loved horses. On Jack's birthday, his father got him a puppy. Jack was very unhappy. He said, "Father, I want a pony!"

His father said, "Son, you are very young to have a pony. Take good care of the puppy and I will get you a pony, once you are a little older."

Feeling sad, Jack left his house and started walking towards the nearby forest. He was so gloomy that he did not see a ditch in the forest and fell in it.

Jack started shouting and crying, loudly. Now, the puppy had followed Jack to the forest. When he saw Jack fall, he ran home and started yelping before Jack's father. The father understood that something was wrong. He followed the puppy to the forest and pulled Jack out of the ditch.

Jack understood that his puppy had saved him. He happily hugged the puppy!

19. The Cat and Venus

Once, a cat liked a young man. She pleaded with Venus, the Goddess of Love, "Oh Venus! Please change me into a woman."

Venus agreed and changed the cat into a beautiful woman. When the young man saw the beautiful woman, he liked her. So, he married her and took her home.

Now Venus wanted to check if the cat in her changed form had also changed her habits of life. So one day, Venus let down a mouse in the middle of the room.

The young woman saw the mouse. She had forgotten that she was no more a cat. So she started crawling up from the couch and chasing the mouse, wanting to eat it.

On seeing that the young woman had not changed her old nature, Venus was very disappointed. Venus said, "You will never give up your old habits!" and changed her back into a cat.

20. A Good Beginning

It was snowing everywhere and the houses were full of Christmas decorations, with rich smell of plum cakes everywhere.

A little boy stood outside his house, waiting for Santa Claus to give him gifts. He was the youngest of the eight siblings, and in all the confusion, his parents had forgotten his Christmas gift.

Immediately, a splendid horse carriage drew up at his door. A man dressed in furs from head to toe, stepped out and greeted the boy. The boy said, "Are you Santa Claus? Where is my gift?"

"Dear boy, I am January. And, I have a gift for you," saying this, January pulled out the loveliest, furriest and the softest hat that the boy had ever seen. The boy thanked and hugged him and ran inside to show his family the wonderful gift.

January thought, "Well, I have begun this New Year happily," and continued his journey further on.

21. A Short Stay

Several boys stood by the melting pond of ice, wondering what to do. "A play! Let's call our parents and bring plenty of eatables! " said a boy.

They agreed on the play and were planning it, when a man dressed in bright clothes, carrying many bags, approached them.

He set up a tent with bright streamers, and soon tables, chairs, food and drinks appeared as if by magic. Their parents also arrived! Everything happened so fast that the boys had to think of a short play very quickly. The play and the eatables were enjoyed thoroughly by all.

A boy asked the man, "Thank you, Sir, for all your help. Who are you?"

"I am February. After the cold January, I wanted you all to enjoy yourselves," he replied.

"I have a short stay, so I must be on my way," said February. He collected his things, and left.

22. A Good Start

"I hate March," said a boy, who had to go to a faraway school. "No March, no school!"

Hearing a sound, he turned around. There was a man wearing glasses, with a bunch of violets in his button-hole. He smiled at the boy.

"So, you hate school? Your parents only want the best for you. Look at your new things," said the man, looking at the boy's packed luggage. "Study well. Your parents will be proud of you. "

"Who may you be, Sir?" asked the boy, finding the man a little strange.

"I am March!" the man said. "You know, each time winter is over, I find it a little difficult to start, but it always turns out to be good, after all."

The boy listened to him and grew up into a great scholar, making his parents really proud of him. He smiles, each time he remembers March.

23. Jack and Magic

Jack lived with his mother, an old witch called Hilda, in Magic Land.

One day, Jack requested his mother to send him away to faraway lands, using magic. Hilda agreed, but warned Jack to be careful.

Jack flew high up in the air. Cool wind caressed his face as he crossed the river and the countryside. He was delighted to see the majestic mountains and the great seas.

Many hours later, hungry and thirsty, Jack landed in a valley of flowers. This was the home of an evil wizard, Fred.

Fred was happy to see him and roared, "Ha! Ha! Ha! You will stay with me as my servant now."

Unknown to both, Hilda had been watching over her son in a crystal ball. She clicked her finger, and in a snap Jack was back home!

24. The Bowman and The Lion

Once there was a very skilful bowman who would shoot arrows at lightning speed. Once he went to the mountains to challenge the animals for a game.

All the animals knew that the bowman was an expert in shooting arrows. They all ran away and hid themselves. The lion accepted the challenge.

The bowman took out an arrow at once and said to the lion, "I am sending you my messenger, this arrow."

The bowman shot the arrow and wounded the lion. The lion roared in pain and backed off from the game. He ran in great fear. A fox that had seen it all happen told the lion, "This was just the first attack. You cannot run away like a coward!"

The lion roared, "Your words don't help me at this moment. If the arrow has harmed me so much, imagine the harm the bowman himself would do!"

25. The Three Important People

One day, in a village school, the teacher called three people to meet the students.

The first person was a king. He was dressed in fine robes and a crown. His family had ruled the kingdom for thousands of years.

The second was a merchant. He had started working hard at a very young age and thus, became successful.

The third was an old man in tattered clothes. He cleaned the streets. However, he was unemployed and homeless now.

"Who is most important of them all?" asked the teacher.

Some students said, "The king, as he makes rules for everyone."

Others said, "The merchant, since he worked hard to achieve this position."

However, the teacher said, "The cleaner is important too, for if he didn't clean the streets, we would have a dirty village."

The children understood that everyone is important in their own ways.

26. The Extra Weight

Long ago, some sailors were sailing on a ship. Their ship was loaded with very heavy materials like iron and wood. Thus, the sailors were unable to turn the ship.

Luckily, the wind started taking the ship towards the port. The captain of the ship said to his sailors, "Let us throw the extra iron and wood into the sea. Then the ship will become lighter and will start moving faster."

The sailors threw the extra material into the sea.

Suddenly, a storm rose in the sea. The waves in the sea started rising very high. Since the ship had become light, it started moving from one side to the other in the high waves.

The ship completely tilted to one side and all the sailors drowned in the sea. If the captain had not acted hastily and kept the extra weight on the ship, it would not have drowned.

27. The Gentle Mermaid

In a clear blue ocean there lived many little fish. This school of fish lived a carefree life, doing as they pleased. Unknown to all dangers, they swam together in a group.

One day, they heard a huge crashing sound in the ocean. All the underwater creatures went to investigate the newest member of the ocean. They thought it was an enemy and went to fight it. But the dolphin advised them to stay away from it, lest it caught them. However, some brave sea folk went closer to inspect, and they saw a human figure. And then to their greatest disbelief, they saw that its lower body was a fish's tail. The wise octopus then told everyone that this mystical creature was a mermaid.

The mermaid begged, "Please allow me to stay here, I will not do any harm to your beautiful sea."

All the creatures welcomed the gentle mermaid lovingly.

28. A Flock of Birds

A flock of birds always stayed together. Thus, when one found some tasty seeds she called the others too. Soon, they were all pecking seeds and eating peacefully.

Sadly, a hunter saw the birds together and threw his net over them. All the birds were trapped in the net. The hunter left the birds to collect some logs.

The birds were struggling to get free. Then, suddenly, the entire flock flew up together, taking the net with them. They reached the top of the tree. There, the net got stuck on the branches of the tree and was ripped. Thus, the birds were free.

Near the tree, the hunter watched the birds in the sky. He thought, "If all the birds decide to help each other like that, I will never be able to catch a single bird again! Each bird is small and delicate, but together, they lifted such a heavy net!"

29. The Three Wishes

Once, the Lord went to a rich man's house and asked to stay the night. But, the rich man refused.

The Lord then went to a poor man's hut. The poor man treated Him with utmost hospitality. The Lord was pleased and granted him three wishes - eternal happiness, health and food for a lifetime and a house.

When the rich man found out, he immediately went to the Lord. He said, "Please stay at my house next time." The Lord agreed and granted him any three wishes.

On his way back, the rich man's horse slipped. So, he wished him dead. Consequently, he had to walk in the heat with the saddle. He said in frustration, "I wish my lazy wife would get stuck on this saddle!" Then, his wife forced him to use the third wish to get her off the saddle. Thus, he wasted all the three wishes!

30. Mother and Son

Once upon a time, there lived a poor little boy. The boy's father was in the army. A few months ago, his father had to go to the border, as there was a war. Unfortunately, he was killed in the war. The boy and his mother were shattered by the loss. They changed their way of living and the boy's mother worked hard, so that the Boy could continue his studies.

The boy saw that his mother was always sad. He wanted to make his mother happy. Therefore, he saved some money and planned to buy her a gift.

He knew that his mother did not have a good coat. So, he went to the market and bought a coat for his mother. Seeing the coat, his mother hugged him tightly and cried in joy.

This kind thought of the boy was indeed proof of the love of a son for his mother.

31. The Boy and the Sweets

Once, a boy lived with his parents.

One day, the boy reached home from school. His mother had left a tall jar filled with his favourite sweets for him.

The boy washed his hands and ran to the table. He put his hand into the tall jar and grabbed a handful.

However, his hand got stuck in the jar! He could not take his hand out of the jar.

The boy tried to free his hand many times, but failed. Tears filled his eyes now. He tried again, but without any luck. Tears rolled down his cheeks.

A gardener looked through the window. Smiling, he said, "Little boy, just let go off some of the sweets! Then your hand will easily slip out! Take only as much as you can eat."

The boy thanked the gardener and said, "I will never be greedy again!"

1. The Haunted Mill

Once, a brave man worked for a merchant. The merchant was actually a wizard.

The man had been working for the merchant without wages. Finally, the man decided to leave and wanted his wages. The merchant told him he would have to live in the mill for a night to get his wages.

In reality, the merchant carried out his magic tricks in the mill. The villagers thought that there was a ghost in the mill.

The man agreed and went with the miller to a room.

When the man was in the room, food appeared out of thin air. Suddenly, the lights dimmed. Just then, the man felt something hit his ear. He hit back bravely and strongly.

In the morning, the miller thanked the man. For, the mill was no longer haunted and the wizard was hurt and ran away. Thus, the man took over his business.

2. If Only I Could Shudder

Once a dim-witted young man heard his brother say, "I can do everything but tasks that give a shudder." His brother was referring to frightening tasks.

Since then, the young man uttered, "If only I could shudder!" People helped him, thinking it was easy to frighten someone.

First came the priest, dressed up as a ghost. The young man was not scared. He thought the ghost was a robber and pushed him from the church building. Alas! The priest broke his leg but the young man uttered, "If only I could shudder!"

On somebody's advice, the young man stayed at a place where seven hanging bodies shook in the wind. He thought they must be cold; so he set up a fire. The young man was annoyed when their clothing caught fire and hung them back! He uttered, "If only I could shudder!"

A king challenged him that he had to stay in a haunted castle for three days. If he was not scared, he would marry the princess. On the first day, there were wild cats and dogs that tried to haunt him. But he cut them into pieces.

The second day, he encountered skeletons but our young man played with the skulls.

The third day, he came across a coffin. He cuddled with the dead body to make it warm. When the dead body was revived, it tried to kill the young man. But he locked it back in the coffin and uttered, "If only I could shudder!"

The king married the young man to the princess.

One day, the princess brought icy water and splashed it on the young man as he slept. He immediately awoke, trembling; "Now I know what it means to shudder!"

However, the young man never understood what it meant to shudder in fear!

3. The Fairy's Gift

Once upon a time, there lived a king. He also had a beautiful garden in his palace. His favourite tree was a magical apple tree. It bore juicy red apples. The tree was a gift from a fairy. The king had rescued this fairy from an evil wizard. The king forbade anyone to pluck and eat the fruit from the tree.

The king had three daughters. One day, the youngest daughter of the king was wandering in the garden. She was tempted on seeing the juicy apples. Despite her father's warning, she plucked the fruit and ate it and disappeared!

The king learned that his daughter had eaten the apple. He called the fairy to help get his daughter back. The fairy came. She said, "I will get her back, but destroy the tree!"

The king agreed sadly. The fairy brought back the princess. The magic tree was destroyed.

4. The Young Man and the Dragon

Once upon a time, a young man was wandering over the countryside. He came across an empty castle. He entered the castle and saw it was fit for a king.

The young man went through the castle. Near the dungeons he heard someone singing softly. He went forward and saw that the voice belonged to a princess. She told him she was a prisoner.

A three-headed dragon guarded the dungeon. To rescue the princess, the dragon would have to be put to sleep. The young man decided to search the castle.

The young man met an elf in the castle. The elf gave him a flute. He told the young man to play it to put the dragon to sleep. The young man played the flute to the dragon. Thus, he put the dragon to sleep and the princess could escape. The princess married the young man.

5. Mountain Kingdom

Once upon a time, there lived a young king. He ruled a magical mountain kingdom. The king once visited a village. However, he lost his magic ring that could take him back to his castle.

The king wandered through the forest. He came across three quarrelling giants. They were trying to divide three things. They had a magic cloak that made a person invisible. Then, they had magic boots that could take a person anywhere. The third was a sword that followed its master's orders and killed people on its own.

The clever king offered to help the giants divide the property. He wore the cloak and became invisible. Then, the king wore the magic boots. He wished to go to his mountain kingdom. At once, he was transported there magically.

The angry giants kept fighting over the sword. Suddenly, a giant shouted, "Bury!" The sword buried itself and was lost.

6. Jupiter and the Farmer

Long ago, Jupiter wanted to rent out his farm. So he sent Mercury to advertise for the farm.

Farmers from everywhere gathered together at the market place to hear the announcement.

The farmers thought that it was too expensive. Then one bold farmer from the crowd decided to hire the farm. The deal was closed between Jupiter and the farmer.

Now whatever the farmer planted grew well. Be it the cold of winter or the heat of summer or the rains, that year the farmer had a good harvest. Even his neighbours were surprised at the yield.

This made the farmer proud and lazy. But the next year, the weather changed and all he planted was in vain. Then the farmer realised that without hard work, the results will never be good. He would only get divine blessings after putting in hard work.

7. The Raven Prince

Once upon a time, there lived a young queen. The queen had a little son. One day, the little son was crying. The queen tried hard to stop the baby's crying, but nothing could stop his crying.

The queen was standing near the window. There were ravens flying around the palace. The tired queen opened the window. She wished that her son were a raven and fly away. Then, she could get some rest.

As soon as the queen spoke these words, her little son turned into a raven and flew away.

The son remained a raven for many years. He lived in a dark forest.

The sorrowful queen took the help of a fairy to find her son. The fairy took her to the forest. Then, she gave a magic potion to the raven. He turned human again. The queen was overjoyed to see her son again.

8. The Enchanted Wood

One day, a young man wandered into a forest. He decided to rest under a tree. He had barely closed his eyes, when the tree spoke to him. The tree told the young man about the princess who was a prisoner in the enchanted woods.

To free the princess, the young man would have to follow certain rules. He had to wait without food or water for three days. He should be awake when the princess rode by in her carriage.

The young man followed the rules till noon on the first day. However, he was very hungry and ate a lot of food. Then, he fell asleep as the princess came by.

The same happened on the second day. The princess left a note for the young man to rescue her. On the third day, the young man followed all the rules and finally rescued the princess from the enchanted woods.

9. The Mortar and the Pestle

Once, a peasant found a mortar, made of gold, in his field. He decided to present it to the king. His daughter asked him not to do so. She told him the king would ask for the pestle, too.

Still, the peasant went with the gold mortar to the king. The king asked for a pestle. When the peasant could not give him the pestle, he was put in prison. The peasant kept crying and talking about of his daughter. He was brought before the king. The peasant told him of her warning.

The king decided to test her wisdom. He asked the daughter to come to the palace not riding, nor walking. If she succeeded, the king would marry her.

The daughter came to the palace wrapped in a fishing net that was dragged by a donkey. Satisfied, the king married the wise daughter and freed her father.

10. The Robbers and the Donkeys

One day, a traveller went on a journey. He loaded one donkey with a sack of money and the other with a sack of grains and left.

The donkey that had the sack of money on him walked with his head held high. He was very proud to carry money on his back. He walked so fast that the bell around his neck rang loudly and clearly. The second donkey that was carrying grains walked behind the first donkey quietly.

When the traveller and his donkeys reached a lonely road, many robbers jumped out from the bushes. The traveller tried to fight with them. But the robbers wounded the donkey that was carrying the money and stole the money sack.

The donkey that was carrying the grains was left unhurt. He saw the wounded donkey and said, "Friend, you should not have been haughty and made all this noise."

11. The Golden Road

Once upon a time, a young prince lived with his father, the king. The king thought that the prince wanted to kill him. The prince could not prove his innocence, thus, the king banished him from his kingdom.

The prince wandered far and wide. He rescued a princess who was a prisoner in an enchanted castle. Then, he promised to return in a year and marry her.

Meanwhile, a minister told the king that the prince was indeed innocent. It was the court jester, who wanted to kill the king.

The king wanted his son back now. He specially built a golden road and instructed the servants that only the real prince would come by that road. All other people took a side road.

Then, one day, the prince and the princess came by the golden road, without even noticing it. The king welcomed them. They all lived happily ever after.

12. The Dog's House

Once, a dog wandered in the lanes of the town all day. He would think every day, "I will make a house for myself soon."

As time passed, winter set in. The dog felt very cold and looked for a place to live in. He found a place and curled up into very little space to keep himself warm.

The dog thought, "Ah! I can fit in very little space. I must be very small."

The dog lived in that corner throughout the winter.

Soon, summer returned. The dog moved to a cooler place. He stretched himself to sleep in a larger space, as sleeping in a small and tight space made him feel hot.

The dog said, "Now, I take up more space. I must be a dog whose size changes. There is no use of making a house. I will not fit in it if I grow larger."

13. The Old Woman and the Kind Boy

Once, there lived a boy who had just one arm.

One cold winter's day, an old woman came to the boy's house. The kind boy opened the door and saw the old woman trembling. He politely invited her to come inside. "Come, old mother, and warm yourself near the fire."

The old woman was glad to accept the offer and she stepped inside. However, she stood too near the fire and her old rags began to burn. She was not aware of it.

The boy saw that the old woman's rags were on fire. He was scared, unable to do anything. Then, he looked around for a bucket of water and found one. He splashed water on the old woman and put the flames out.

The old woman thanked the boy for saving her life. She was actually a fairy. She blessed him and the boy got his other arm!

14. The Boy's Village

Once, a boy lived in a village with his parents. The boy loved his village, its market and its church.

One day, his father announced, "I have got a very good job in the city. So, we will have to leave the village forever."

The boy was very upset and cried all night. His mother said, "Do not worry, son. You must study hard in the city and earn good money. Then you will easily be able to come back to your village."

The boy understood and worked hard. He grew up and became a rich man. All these years, his desire to go back to his village kept growing.

Finally, he collected all his money and went back to his village. His eyes were filled with tears when he saw the same market, church and met his old friends.

He bought a huge house there and lived there forever.

15. The Good Boys

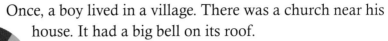

Once, a boy lived in a village. There was a church near his house. It had a big bell on its roof.

The sound of the bell was music to the ears of everybody in the village. The boy and his friends played near the bell every day and enjoyed its music.

One day, the rope of the bell broke and it fell down. The villagers blamed the boys who were playing there.

Everybody was very sad as nobody could hear the music of the bell. So, the boys decided to buy a new rope and tie the bell again.

They went to every home in the village and collected money. They gathered enough money in a week's time. Then, they bought a new rope and tied the bell to the roof again.

The villagers gathered near the church on hearing the sound and thanked the boys.

16. Long Bony Fingers

Once, there was a naughty boy. He was very fond of reading but spent most of his time reading stories of horror. He then played tricks on the younger boys, not realising that it scared them.

His father told him not to do so, but the boy did not pay any attention. One day, his father planned to teach him a lesson.

The boy went to the library and forgot that he had to go home on time. On his way back, the road was lonely and it was dark. The boy walked fast. Suddenly he heard a creepy voice, "I will prick you with my long bony fingers."

Scared, the boy started running but tripped in the dark. Then he saw a figure coming towards him. The poor boy screamed in horror, but then discovered it was his father.

Now he decided not to trouble his friends again.

17. The Brave Boy and the Cruel Men

Once upon a time, there was a man. He wanted to become rich very soon. He went to his village and told people that he had a flourishing business in the city. He told the parents of little children, that in his spare time, he would like to teach their children.

Many people believed him and sent their children to him. One day, a boy followed the man. He saw the man entering an old, broken building. There were more men inside waiting for him. They all went to a hall.

The boy was shocked to see all the children tied up with ropes. The men hurt the children, injured their hands or feet and forced them to beg.

The boy came back and told everything to the village headman. All the villagers were furious at this news and ran with sticks in their hands. The greedy men were caught and punished. The brave boy saved the other children and told them, "Don't ever talk to strangers!"

18. The Fairies

Once, there was a poor boy. He lived alone at a farm and worked hard to earn his living. He did all the work but his master was never happy. He did not give him enough food to eat. But the boy respected him and always prayed to God to help him.

One day, the boy received a letter. He asked the master's son to read the letter. There was a surprise! He had been invited by the fairies to the New Year party. The boy was confused but the master's son encouraged him to go. He even gave him nice clothes to wear.

The boy went to the party and had a very nice time. He danced and ate to his heart's content. The fairies tried to make him happy. Finally, he was tired and fell asleep.

He woke up in a beautiful house and led a happy life.

19. Thumbling

Once, there lived a carpenter and his wife. They had everything but were sad, as they did not have any children. God listened to their prayers and blessed them with a child but it was only as big as a thumb. So they named him Thumbling.

The parents loved their child. One day, the carpenter was going to the forest to cut wood. He wanted his wife to come in the afternoon and help him. Before leaving, the wife asked Thumbling to look after the house.

When everybody was asleep, two thieves entered the carpenter's house. Little Thumbling was surprised to see the thieves steal valuables and grains.

Thumbling quietly ran to the neighbour's house and told him about the thieves. The neighbour called some friends and came to the carpenter's house. The thieves started running but everybody followed them and beat them badly. Everybody was very proud of Thumbling.

20. The Flea and the Wrestler

Once, a wrestler lived in a small town. He believed in God Hercules. Every day, he prayed to Hercules for strength and happiness.

One day, he was preparing himself for a wrestling match. Just then, a flea came buzzing around him. The wrestler was not wearing his shoes. Thus, the flea bit him on his toe. The wrestler screamed in pain and started praying to Hercules to help him. After a while, the flea hopped on his toe again and bit him for a second time. The wrestler screamed loudly.

The wrestler continued praying. However, Hercules did not help him. The wrestler cried and said, "O Hercules! If you did not help me against a little flea, how can I hope for your help against stronger opponents?"

Suddenly, Hercules appeared. He said, "Dear man, I will only help you if you do your best to help yourself."

21. The Fisherman and God

There once lived a fisherman who was very mean. He never helped anybody in need, for he was very selfish and arrogant.

One day, while he was out fishing, a storm broke out and his boat was caught in the waves. He tried his best to sail his boat towards the shore, but in vain. Soon, his boat began to fill with water. He prayed to God, "God please save my life. From now on I shall help everyone who is in need."

Soon, the storm calmed and he reached the shore. He was a changed man now. He began lending a helping hand to anyone and everyone who needed help.

The fisherman started praying more often. He was thankful, that at the time he needed help the most, God had helped him. He kept his part of the promise to God and helped every needy person he came across.

22. The Magical Pear

One day, an old man was selling pears. He came near the house of a poor couple.

The old lady who was standing in the porch saw his tired face and offered him a glass of water. Happy at her kindness, the old pear seller came in to drink water. He was indeed very thirsty.

While leaving, he handed a pear to the old couple. He asked them to share the pear and their dream would be fulfilled. The poor couple did not believe in magic, but the pear looked so delicious that they shared it.

The next day, while they were talking, they realised that both had the same dream the previous night. Both had dreamed of living in a huge house.

Later that day, when the old lady's husband was ploughing his garden, he found a metal chest full of gold coins. The pear seller's words had come true.

23. The Little Boy and the Puppy

Once, a farmer wanted to sell puppies.

A little boy went to the farmer and said, "Sir, can I buy one of your puppies?"

The farmer said, "Of course! But it will cost lots of money."

The boy had very little money, so he said, "Can I just see them?"

The farmer whistled and the puppies came running out. The last one was limping.

The little boy asked, "What is wrong with him?"

The farmer said, "He has injured one leg. He cannot run and play."

The little boy's eyes lit up. He sat down and rolled up his pants. He had steel braces and a special shoe. He said, "I can't run and play either. We will understand each other."

The farmer said, "You may have him for free. He will be your best friend. I am glad he's got you."

The little boy walked home happily with his puppy.

24.The Thief and the Lamp

Once, a thief went to the church at night. He wanted to steal the gifts that people offered to God. It was very dark inside. He went to the altar and lit his lamp with the God's fire. Then, he used the lamp to steal all the riches from the church.

God was very upset with the theft. He said, "I gave him fire to light the lamp but this wicked man stole from the church."

God's angels cursed the thief, for he had hurt God. They said, "This wicked man broke God's trust. He will soon get punished."

Also, they forbade all mankind from using the God's fire.

The thief met with an accident and died after a few days. However, even today, one is not allowed to light the lamps with the sacred fire in temples and churches.

Thus, the entire mankind got punished for one man's fault.

25. The Rich Man's Utensils

Once, a rich man lived in a village. One day, a villager borrowed some utensils from the rich man. After some days, he returned more than he had borrowed and said, "Some utensils gave birth to new ones. So, the number has increased."

The rich man was greedy and therefore accepted them. Sometime later, the villager again borrowed some utensils and did not return them for a long time.

The rich man waited patiently, because he hoped to get more utensils than he gave. One month later, he went to the villager's house and asked, "Why did you not return my utensils?"

The villager replied, "All your utensils died last week."

The rich man shouted, "Liar! How can the utensils die?"

The villager replied, "If the utensils can give birth to new utensils, then they can die also."

The rich man understood that he had been fooled, but kept quiet.

26. The Hunter and the Bear

Once, a hunter lived in a forest. One morning, he saw a bear climb the mountain. He wanted to shoot him, but the way to the mountain was very narrow with a valley on both sides. The bear would fall in the valley on being shot and would not be useful to the hunter.

So, the hunter waited for the bear to reach the mountain. After sometime, he saw a small bear come down the mountain from the other side.

The hunter thought, "The passage is very narrow and both the bears cannot cross each other. They will fight and fall in the valley."

However, when both bears reached each other, the big bear sat down. The smaller bear climbed on his back and crossed over. The big bear got up and walked up the mountain.

The hunter was surprised to see that animals, unlike humans, co-operate and live peacefully.

27. The Bald Men and the Comb

It was a beautiful evening. A bald man went out for a walk, enjoying the cool breeze.

Suddenly something on the ground struck his foot. It was a comb!

Just as he bent down to pick it up, a stranger called out to him, "I saw it, too! We must share it!"

The bald man smiled, "Of course, I will share it with you, but I do not think it will help you at all!" Then, the bald man opened his palm to show the stranger the comb.

The stranger silently looked at the comb. He could not use it, for he too was bald.

The bald man said, "The Gods wanted to give us something good, but Fate did not want the gift to be useful. Instead of giving us hair, he gave us a round moon on our heads."

He threw the comb and walked back home.

28. Diogenes and the Ferryman

Diogenes was a great thinker who lived in Greece. He had a sharp mind, so many people respected him.

Once, during his travels, Diogenes found himself before a stream in flood. He could not cross over. The stream flowed swiftly by, carrying branches and stones. Diogenes watched helplessly.

The kind ferryman, who often rowed people across the stream in his boat, saw Diogenes. "Come!" said the ferryman, "I will row you safely across!"

Diogenes was very thankful. The kind ferryman told him, "You don't need to pay me."

Just then the ferryman saw an angry and mean traveller. The ferryman rowed his boat to help him, too.

Seeing this, Diogenes said, "Now I can see that you are not really a kind and good man. Helping people is just a habit for you!"

The ferryman was shocked and hurt to hear Diogenes. He understood that not everybody understands kindness.

29. True and False Dreams

One day, Apollo requested God for a special power. He wanted to see the future and tell people on the Earth about it.

Since Apollo was God's favourite minister, God granted his wish. Now, Apollo became a fortune-teller and became popular. People worshipped him the most. This made him proud. God did not like it and wanted to teach him a lesson.

God made dreams and told people their future in sleep. Slowly, people realised that they could see the future in sleep and did not need Apollo. They stopped worshipping him.

Now, Apollo realised his mistake and apologised to God. He promised to be polite and humble in future. He stopped telling people their future all the time.

God forgave him and showed people false dreams in sleep. After some time, people realised that all their dreams were not true. Now people stopped trying to know their future.

30. A Crocodile and a Fisherman

Once, a fisherman lived with his wife. They were sad because they did not have a baby.

One day, the fisherman went to the river and threw his nets. Suddenly, he saw a crocodile's egg on the bank.

"Oh poor egg," thought the fisherman, "I shall take it home!"

The fisherman's wife was happy with the egg. She said, "It will be like a child to us!"

Soon, a dark grey-green crocodile was born. The fisherman and his wife took good care of him.

Soon, the crocodile became so big that the couple put him back into the same river where the fisherman had found him.

Every day, the fisherman visited the river to feed the crocodile and catch fish. One day, the crocodile by mistake bit the fisherman. He found him tasty. Thus, he opened his mouth and swallowed him. The poor fisherman was killed for meddling with nature!

1. The Tiger

Once there was a little boy called Harry. He loved tigers. He had tiger toys, posters and blankets and watched tiger videos.

As Harry's birthday drew near, he asked his parents to gift him a tiger.

On the day of his birthday, Harry received a hat from his grandparents, a pair of socks from his uncle but did not receive any gift from his parents. He was hurt and started crying bitterly. Then, his father took him to the garage and showed him a big box. Inside the box was a tiger. Harry hugged the tiger in joy. The tiger, in turn, licked his face.

The same day Harry bought a collar for the tiger so that he could take him out for a walk.

That evening Harry took the tiger to the park for a walk. He wanted to show the tiger to all his friends. But, all his friends got scared and ran away on seeing the tiger.

The next day, Harry took the tiger to school. The same thing happened there and everyone jumped out of the classroom, including the teacher who had taught them about tigers.

Harry thought that his dear granny would be pleased to see the tiger, but she too screamed and ran away on seeing it.

Harry came back home upset and told his father about the problem.

Harry's father immediately made a call. In a few minutes, a man came with a big lorry and took the tiger back to Africa. Then, Harry and his father went to a pet shop and picked up a cute little puppy.

Everyone liked the little puppy. Harry's granny even gave him dog food, every time he visited her.

Since then, every summer, Harry and his family went to Africa to visit the tigers.

2. The King's Dream

Once there lived a good king. He often visited a hermit for advice.

One night, the king dreamt that his minister was enjoying himself, sitting in a green field and thinking deeply.

The next night the king had another dream. This time he saw a poor hermit on fire.

The king was puzzled by his dreams. So he asked the hermit the meaning.

The wise hermit replied, "Sometimes God speaks through dreams. Sometimes your minister is so tired, he wants to be a hermit. He wants to go away from the noise and live in the quiet fields!"

"The hermit always lives alone. Sometimes he longs to see the beautiful palace, and enjoy life for a little while!" the hermit continued.

"However, each loves his own life. But the minister loves the palace life, whereas the hermit loves his quietness. People cannot live the other's life for long."

3. The Little Flower Seller

Once, there lived a poor boy. His father was a flower seller.

It was Christmas time. The boy too wanted to celebrate Christmas with his family. However, his father was very ill and there was no money at home.

Thus, the boy went to his garden and plucked some flowers. Then, he went to the market and cried out loudly, "Come and buy my wonderful flowers."

The boy shouted for an hour but sadly no one heard him!

Suddenly, a lady stopped by him. She saw his flowers and bought all of them. Then she said, "You are a very good son! I am December, the Queen of Good Cheer. I bless you that you will grow up to be a kind and happy man!"

Then she disappeared!

The boy ran home to celebrate Christmas with his family! Many years later, he grew up to be a wonderful doctor!

4. The Useful Scissors

Once, a pair of scissors lived in a shop. The other tools in the shop made fun of it, for it looked ugly.

The poor scissors was very sad.

Then, one day, a man bought the scissors. The scissors was not sure what he did and was scared. It wondered what the future held!

When the man reached his shop, he took the scissors out of its box. Then he cut a piece of cloth with it.

In a few minutes, the scissors saw that the man had made a beautiful pink shirt with it. The scissors understood that the man was a tailor.

In the evening, a little boy came to the shop with his mother. The boy was excited to see his pink shirt and went home happily.

The scissors was very happy. She realised that it is one's work that brings joy in people's life, not looks!

9. The Wishing Tray

There was once a boy who had lost his parents. He lived with his uncle and aunt. Sadly, his aunt did not give him good food to eat.

One day, his aunt invited some children. She cooked very delicious dishes for all of them.

The children were very happy and enjoyed the feast. But the boy was sad because his aunt did not give him that food. That day, the boy cried a lot and slept. In his dream, he saw a fairy.

The fairy said, "Don't worry, my child. In the morning, you will see a small tray near you. Whenever you want to eat anything, just wish for it and it will appear on the tray."

The boy was happy and ate wonderful food. When he shared the food with his aunt and uncle, his aunt was ashamed of her bad ways. She took good care of him, thereafter.

10. The Gold Ass

Once, there lived a peasant. He worked hard, but still could not earn enough to take care of his family.

The peasant had an ass, which he used to carry wood from the forest.

One day, the peasant fell ill. Whatever little money he had, was spent on his treatment. The peasant's wife wanted to sell the ass, but the peasant did not allow that.

The peasant's wife prayed for her husband's good health and happiness. That night while going to sleep, she saw a bright light appear in front of her. Then she heard a voice say, "Your ass is extraordinary. If you pat him thrice on his back, he spits out gold coins."

The wife immediately tried it out and the ass spit out gold coins.

Soon, the peasant was well again. He became very rich and took good care of his family. They all lived happily.

11. The Boy and the Carnival

Once, a boy lived with his poor parents in a small town. The town had a beautiful church and organised a Christmas carnival every year.

The boy wanted to go to the carnival but did not have good clothes to wear. He asked his parents for new clothes.

The father said, "Son, we don't have money. But, God always listens to children. So, pray that my goods are sold and I can take you to the carnival."

The boy understood and prayed hard. God listened to the boy's prayers as all his father's goods were sold. That evening, his father bought new clothes for the family and took them to the carnival.

It was a beautiful evening. The boy enjoyed many rides, dances and balloons. He and his family ate many delicacies and his parents bought him many gifts. The boy thanked God and since then prayed regularly.

12. The Magic Club

Once, there was a small village. All the villagers lived in peace and harmony. They worked hard in their fields and grew plenty of crops.

The people of the neighbouring village were very lazy. They did not want to work and always asked the farmers of the other village to help them. One year, the hard-working farmers refused to help the lazy farmers.

Now, people who are lazy do not easily change their habits. The lazy villagers planned to steal the grains from the storehouse of the other village. One night, a group of villagers quietly crept into the headman's storehouse. The guards had seen them entering. Nobody knew that the headman had a magic club that would beat anybody when the headman ordered it to.

The guards called the headman. He came with his club and ordered it to beat the villagers. The villagers never dared to come back.

13. The Greedy Cow

Once, there was a milkman. He had some cows and buffaloes. One of the cows was his favourite. He fed his family members on her milk.

One day, his eldest son took the cattle to the fields. In the evening, the son asked the cow if she had had enough. The cow said, "I am full."

At night, the milkman asked the cow the same question and she said, "I am starving."

The milkman scolded his son and threw him out of the house.

The next two days, the cow repeated the same behaviour with the other two sons. The milkman threw them out as well.

Now he himself took the cow to feed on fresh, green plants. When he asked her later, the cow said, "I am starving."

The milkman understood that his cow was greedy. He brought his sons back home and never pampered the ungrateful cow again.

14. The Lion and the Dog

One day, a lion was hunting in the forest. Just then, he heard the sound of horses galloping towards him. The lion understood that hunters were coming after him. He started running.

Sadly, the hunters caught him and flung a net on him.

The hunters were tired and hungry. Thus, they tied the lion's net to a tree and sat down to eat. Soon they all fell asleep under the trees nearby.

The hunters had also fed the dogs. One of the hunters' dogs was very kind. He offered the lion some food. The lion cried out, "Oh! How can I eat? My poor family will be hungry and waiting for me!"

The dog felt very sad for the lion. He tried to cut the ropes and the net with his teeth. The lion tried too and soon he was free! He thanked the dog and ran off to his family.

15. The Old Tree

Once, a farmer had a beautiful orchard of trees.

One day, the farmer saw that in the corner of the orchard, there was an old tree. Just then, his neighbour, the woodcutter came to meet him.

The woodcutter exclaimed, "Look at this old tree. It is unlucky to have such a tree. Cut it down at once!"

Just then, the farmer's little son came running and said, "Father, please don't cut that tree! It is the home of so many birds and creatures. The sparrows have their nest in it and there are eggs in the nest. If you cut the tree, the eggs will break and there will be no baby sparrows. The squirrel also lives there. His father is unwell and cannot move. If you cut the tree, the squirrel's father will die!"

The farmer understood that the old tree was actually very valuable, and he never cut it!

16. The King and the Beggar

Once, a rich man lived in a village with his wife and son.

One day, the king came to the rich man's house. The son spoke very politely to the king and the king presented him with a gold coin.

The next day, a beggar came to the rich man's house to ask for alms. He stood at the door and called out, "Please give me some food. I have not eaten for two days."

The son ran out and shouted, "Oh no! Go away! I don't have any food for you."

Just then, the rich man came out with a plate full of food. He said, "Here, please take this."

The beggar took the food and thanked him.

Then, the rich man said to his son, "You spoke so politely with the king. The beggar is also a child of God. You should speak politely to him, too!"

17. The Harpist and the Princess

There once lived a poor boy, whose parents had died when he was young. They had left a musical harp for him.

The boy loved to play his harp and soon became an expert. Everyone who heard him, gave him money.

One day, an evil magician heard his music. He felt jealous and shouted, "Boy, until a princess calls you the best musician in the world, you will look ugly!"

The boy was very sad as his face became ugly. Now no one came near him. Thus, he moved from one place to another, begging for food.

One day, as he passed by a palace, he played a beautiful tune. The princess heard the sweet music and called out, "You may look ugly, but you are the best musician in the world!"

The boy lost his ugliness. The princess fell in love with him and they both were married soon.

18. The Man and the Writer

A man knew someone who was writing his first book. This writer invited the man over for tea.

After tea, the writer started reading his book. The man was first bored, then he got tired and finally, he was very annoyed. But, he kept silent, not wanting to be rude.

The writer kept saying: "I am such a great writer and I write so beautifully. No one else can write like me."

The man tried to tell the writer that he had to go home. He had lots of work to finish. But, the writer kept on reading.

When the reading was over and the man was completely exhausted, the writer asked, "I should not praise myself, but don't you think I am the greatest writer in this city?"

The man said tiredly, "I think that you should continue to praise yourself, because no one else is ever going to."

19. The King's Chariot Driver

Once, there lived a proud man with his wife. The man used to drive the chariot of the king.

One day, he said to his wife, "You must come and see me, then you will feel proud of me."

The wife went to see her husband drive the king's chariot. She noticed that he was driving the chariot very arrogantly, whereas the king sat in his chariot calm and composed.

In the evening, when the man returned, his wife said, "I want to leave you."

"Leave me!" exclaimed the man, "You want to leave the king's chariot driver! You are very foolish."

The wife replied to her proud husband, "I came to see you drive the king today. He is the king, yet he is so modest and humble. You are just his driver but you are so arrogant."

The man was very ashamed and became humble from then on.

20. Ferbs and the Lamp

Once, there lived a boy called Ferbs.

One day, Ferbs went to the marketplace. On the way, an old woman stopped him and said, "Please help me to carry this huge sack of coal home."

Ferbs was a kind boy and helped the old woman. However, the old woman was evil. She took Ferbs to her castle in the forest. She made Ferbs her slave.

One day, Ferbs was cleaning the storeroom when he found an old lamp. Ferbs cleaned the lamp and tried to light it. Suddenly, a fairy came out of the lamp.

The fairy at once killed the evil woman. Then she said, "Thank you! The evil woman had captured me and you saved me! Now ask me for three wishes."

Ferbs wished for riches, good food and to go back to his mother.

The fairy fulfilled them all and Ferbs lived happily with his mother ever after!

21. The Coach and the Fly

Once, six strong horses were drawing a coach up a steep hilly road. The coach carried women, children and monks.

Soon the tired and weary group stopped for a break. A fly approached them and buzzed around the horses' ears. He pricked them and annoyed them.

The group started their journey again. The fly believed that he had made the carriage go and moved along. He flew back and forth along the carriage in great hurry. He buzzed about the horses as a sergeant does in a battle.

The fly felt very important and complained that no one else helped the horses except him.

Soon the coach reached the top. The fly buzzed before the coach driver and said, "Dear friend, you may stop and breathe now. I have got you up the hill. Pay me my fare!"

The driver was annoyed by the foolish fly and killed it.

22. The Mighty Tree

Once, there grew a large tree and a little plant side by side. The tree rose high into the sky. The passersby stopped to admire it.

The plant looked small and weak. Nobody took notice of it.

"Look at me," said the tree to the plant, "I stand so boldly in the air. Why don't you stand like me?"

"I may be safer this way," whispered the plant gently.

"Safer!" exclaimed the tree. "So, you think you are safer than I am! No one dare pluck me by the roots or bow my head," he boasted. The plant kept silent.

One evening a big storm arose. Tall mighty trees were uprooted. The little plant tossed and turned but did not break. After the storm had passed there remained no sign of the mighty tree. However, the little plant was seen rocking it head happily in the gentle breeze.

23. Chuck and the Shipbuilders

One day, there was a young boy called Chuck. Everyone in the village knew that Chuck was a good storyteller

One day, Chuck passed by a ship-builder's workshop. The ship-builders requested him for a story. Chuck was silent.

Then, a ship-builder said, "Chuck, we are the mightiest of all on Earth! Everybody else should listen to what we say and do what we ask!"

These words annoyed Chuck. He said, "I know a good story...Before the Earth was made, God made Chaos and Water. God then decided to make Mother Earth. So, he made Earth and asked her to swallow the sea. In the first gulp, the mountains came up. In the second gulp, the plains came up, flat and dry. Earth has not taken a third gulp – if she did, there would be no Water and no ship-builders or ships! So be grateful to God!"

24. The Merchant and his Slippers

Once there was a wealthy, miserly merchant. He wore an old torn pair of slippers.

One day, the merchant visited a public bath and left his slippers outside. On his return he found new slippers there. Thinking that they were a gift, he wore them.

The new slippers belonged to a judge. The merchant was called to the court and was punished for stealing them.

The merchant threw his old slippers out of the window. They fell into a fisherman's net and damaged it. The angry fisherman threw them back and broke the merchant's expensive vase.

Now, the merchant was fed up with his slippers and decided to bury them. However, a neighbour thought that he was burying guns and complained about him. He was called to the court again. In tears, he told the judge the entire story. The kind judge told him that he should not be miserly.

25. Christmas

Once, there lived a boy with his old grandparents.

The boy was excited as Christmas was just a month away! However, his grandfather was a poor farmer and they had little money.

The boy started grazing the neighbour's goats after school. Thus, he collected some money by Christmas. He presented his grandmother with warm stockings and his grandfather with a new pipe.

Then he bought some delicious cakes and sweets for them! On his way back, he met three hungry orphans and happily gave away some food to them. He just kept three sweets for his grandparents and himself.

When he reached home, the boy saw his poor neighbour's little girl crying. He, at once, gave her the leftover sweets.

That night, as the boy slept, God's angels filled his house with good food and lots of toys! God blessed him for being the kindest person on Christmas!

26. The Old Man

Once, an old man lived in a village. The old man's wife had died and his only son went off to the city to study.

All the other villagers often said, "Oh! It is so sad that you are alone in your old age!"

But the old man always said, "Everything happens for the good!"

After some time, the old man's son returned and everyone expressed joy and happiness. The old man thanked them and said, "Whatever happens, happens for the good!"

A few days later the old man's son fell from a horse and broke his leg. The old man still said, "Everything happens for the good!"

After a while, the king's army came to the village to employ young men as soldiers. The old man's son was left behind because of his broken leg. The villagers now realised how true and wise the old man's words were.

27. A Young Man and a Villager

Once, a young man met a villager, who said, "I go to the forest and stand under a mango tree and say a spell. Then, the tree bears lots of ripe mangoes. I will teach you the spell, but don't use it for your own greed, and never tell a lie."

After learning the spell, the young man returned to his own village. Soon, he became a rich man, by selling the mangoes he got through the spell.

The king wanted to know who had taught him the magic. The young man was ashamed that he had learnt the spell from a simple villager. So, he told the king that he had learnt it from a magician.

The king asked him to perform the spell in the royal orchard. However, since the young man had lied, thus, the spell did not work. He was sorry but could never use the mango spell again.

28. The Passenger and the Sailor

Once, a big ship sailed in the sea. One night, there was a big storm. It started raining very heavily.

One scared passenger went to the sailor. He saw that the sailor was very calm and asked him, "I am very scared of dying. Sailor, aren't you?"

The sailor replied, "No, I grew up on ships and my father even died on a ship."

"Why then, did you choose the job as a sailor; are you not afraid that you can also die on the ship?"

The sailor laughed and asked the passenger, "Tell me how your father died?"

The passenger replied, "He died while sleeping."

The sailor asked, "You must be afraid to sleep! If you think I should not work on a ship as it might kill me as it killed my father, then you should also not sleep on a bed or it will kill you!"

29. The Philosopher among the Tombs

Once upon a time, there lived a philosopher. He was intelligent and knowledgeable.

One day, he went to a graveyard. He found two human skeletons, one was of a duke and the other of a common beggar.

The philosopher looked closely at both the skeletons and could not make out the difference between the two. Their bones looked the same.

After spending some time in reasoning he said, "If the body structure of all human beings is made in the same form, then surely the way a man behaves depends on the mind and not the blood and bones."

God made us all equal when he created us. Human beings differentiate on the basis of skin colour, blood and religion. When we die, we all become the same sand. Then no one can differentiate what we were, which religions we belonged to, or from where we came.

30. The Young Boy

Once, there lived a young boy in a village.

One day, on his way to school, the young boy noticed birds chirping, dogs barking, toads croaking and a lot of men talking aloud.

At school, the young boy asked his teacher, "Sir, is it good to talk a lot?"

The teacher answered with an example, "Son, toads and frogs croak night and day, but no one listens to them. The cock on the other hand crows early in the morning and wakes everyone up. It is very important to speak right things at the right time. No one listens to those, who speak without reason, but everyone respects those who speak less but talk sense."

The young boy understood the importance of golden silence.

"Thank you for teaching me such a good lesson, Sir. I will remember this all my life," said the young boy, gratefully to his teacher.

31. All Little Boys

Jupiter, the God of Thunder, had a baby boy.

Jupiter wanted his son to be strong and great. So he called all the Gods for a meeting.

Mars, the God of War, offered to teach the boy to fight. "I will teach him to win every battle," he said.

"I will teach him to make beautiful music," promised Apollo, the God of Poetry and Music.

Hercules, the God of Strength, said he would teach the boy to be strong in body and mind!

However, Cupid, the God of Love, said, "The others may teach the boy wonderful skills. He may be strong, may win battles and play music. However, I will teach him to love! That is the greatest thing! You can get many things using power. But you can get all things through love!"

Jupiter said, "All little boys should love their parents and all the people they meet!"

TITLES IN THIS SERIES

ISBN: 978-93-83202-81-2

ISBN: 978-93-84225-32-2

ISBN: 978-93-84225-33-9

ISBN: 978-93-84625-92-4

ISBN: 978-93-84225-31-5

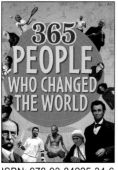

ISBN: 978-93-84225-34-6

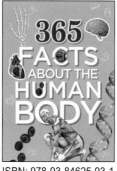

ISBN: 978-93-84625-93-1

ISBN: 978-93-80069-36-4

ISBN: 978-93-81607-49-7

ISBN: 978-81-87107-55-2

ISBN: 978-93-80070-79-7

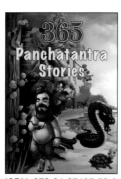

ISBN: 978-81-87107-58-3

ISBN: 978-93-80070-84-1

ISBN: 978-93-80070-83-4

ISBN: 978-81-87107-56-9

ISBN: 978-81-87107-52-1

ISBN: 978-81-87107-53-8

ISBN: 978-81-87107-57-6

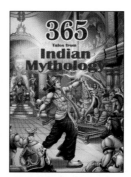

ISBN: 978-81-87107-46-0

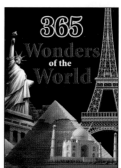

ISBN: 978-93-80069-35-7